Restored
BY GRACE

BROKEN VESSELS, USABLE FOR GOD'S GLORY.

A compilation of short stories of restoration, hope and grace.

STEPHEN H. REED

Restored by Grace

Restored by Grace by Stephen H. Reed
Published by: Burning Bush Media Group

"Scripture quotations taken from the New American Standard Bible®, Copyright ©1960, 1962, 1963, 1968, 1971, 1972, 1973, 1975, 1977, 1995 by The Lockman Foundation   Used by permission."
(www.Lockman.org)

To order single copies or bulk quantities of this book, visit
www.StephenReedMinistries.com
www.fb.me/StephenReedMinistries
or email me at: Info@StephenReedMinistries.com

ISBN: 978-0-9864477-8-5

Printed in the United States of America

Restored by Grace

Table of Contents

Endorsements

"Testimonies have a way of taking the impossible and illuminating hope. This book is a resource of hope. The author, my friend, has years of ministry under his belt in illuminating to literally hundreds of people. The combination of Steve being Steve & the testimonials in this book are an encouraging "lighthouse" in any storm of life."

"This book reminds me of Jesus' own words, recorded for us in Mark 10:27 "But Jesus looked at them and said, "With men it is impossible, but not with God, for with God all things are possible.""

"With God, truly there is always hope!"

Eric Coburn
Senior Pastor, Calvary Chapel
Frisco, TX

"Restored by Grace is a book of hope. The stories in this book are so enthralling that they'll bring hope and inspiration to every reader!"

Sandy Anderson
Founder/President
Build International Ministries

"Grace. There is not a lot of grace in today's world. How do you find it? How do you accept grace? How do you embrace grace? How do you live grace? How do you give grace? Steve Reed shares stories in which we can all identify. Whether it is Ben, Becky, Sam, or Hank, their stories reflect our struggles. The common thread is that God's grace is sufficient. Steve encourages us to be available for that grace."

Bryan Flanagan
CEO of Flanagan Training Group

Restored by Grace is a book anyone can connect with and everyone can learn from. This book can help those who are going through a tough season and is a helpful guide for those trying to help someone in a tough season.

Caleb Beets
Spiritual Formation Pastor
Cottonwood Creek Church
Allen, TX

Appreciation and Dedication

Being grateful doesn't come close to my feelings for Suzanne Reed. I know that when God was forming her in her mother's womb, He knew that He was forming her to be my incredible wife. God knew my every need and gave her to me to care for and protect. I prayed for a long time that God would bless me with someone like her. Godly, focused, giving, sentimental, generous, loving... the list goes on. What a wonderful helpmate she is. Thank you Suzanne for who you are.

I am dedicating this book to all those who are hurting in various forms. I have been honored to work with so many people over the years who have dealt with divorce, loss of a parent, molestation, rape, drug abuse...etc. There are many people who I have helped discover who they really are in the eyes of their Creator.

If you fall into any of these categories, I hope you will be blessed by reading this compendium of stories. Know that you are loved. Be blessed and be a blessing to others with whom you cross paths.

Preface

We live in a broken world. These "breaks" come in many different forms. What might be trivial to some, may be a mountain to others.

We have all heard it said, "You are either going through a crisis, just coming out of a crisis, or about to head into a crisis." The question is, where do you fall in this equation?

This book is based on true life stories of people. I have personally walked alongside each of them, offering help and the tools needed in overcoming their struggles.

As you read this book, you may be able to identify with one or more of the stories. You may know friends, family, business associates, or church members who have struggled with some of these issues.

Know that the purpose of this book is to give hope for the future. You may feel as though you are stuck, or worse, trapped and can't get out, or you are gripped with bitterness or anger against someone who wronged you. Hold on to hope, the true hope of Jesus Christ, and know that there are answers. Some answers can be extremely difficult, and you won't want to take the first step in order to get what you need. Fight for yourself, you are worth it! In God's eyes, you are worth it!!

No one said it better than Zig Ziglar, "You were designed for accomplishment, engineered for success, and endowed with the seeds of greatness."

Now, go and become who God says you are, not the lies the world says about you.

Introduction

"In the beginning God created the heavens and the earth. The earth was formless and void, and darkness was over the surface of the deep, and the Spirit of God was moving over the surface of the waters. Then God said, "Let there be light"; and there was light. God saw that the light was good; and God separated the light from the darkness. God called the light day, and the darkness He called night. And there was evening and there was morning, one day. Then God said, "Let there be an expanse in the midst of the waters, and let it separate the waters from the waters." God made the expanse and separated the waters which were below the expanse from the waters which were above the expanse; and it was so. God called the expanse heaven. And there was evening and there was morning, a second day. Then God said, "Let the waters below the heavens be gathered into one place, and let the dry land appear"; and it was so. God called the dry land earth, and the gathering of the waters He called seas; and God saw that it was good. Then God said, "Let the earth sprout vegetation, plants yielding seed, and fruit trees on the earth bearing fruit after their kind with seed in them"; and it was so. The earth brought forth vegetation, plants yielding seed after their kind, and trees bearing fruit with seed in them, after their kind; and God saw that it was good. There was evening and there was morning, a third day. Then God said, "Let there be lights in the expanse of the heavens to separate the day from the night and let them be for signs and for seasons and for days and years; and let them be for lights in the expanse of the heavens to give light on the earth"; and it was so. God made the two great lights, the greater light to govern the day, and the lesser light to govern the night; He made the stars also. God placed them in the expanse of the heavens to give light on the earth, and to govern the day and the night, and to separate the light

from the darkness; and God saw that it was good. There was evening and there was morning, a fourth day."
Genesis 1:1-19

Our story begins with that of creation by an Infinite God. He is not "a god", He is Thee God, and He is perfect in every way.

Throughout His creation process, everything He did was perfect. Perfect amount of daylight and darkness, perfect amount of land and water. Perfect balance in all of nature, just plain perfect!

God created every living thing, plants, sea creatures, flying animals, and land animals. Then came man created in God's own image. Man had it great!

"Then God said, "Let Us make man in Our image, according to Our likeness; and let them rule over the fish of the sea and over the birds of the sky and over the cattle and over all the earth, and over every creeping thing that creeps on the earth." God created man in His own image, in the image of God He created him; male and female He created them. God blessed them; and God said to them, "Be fruitful and multiply, and fill the earth, and subdue it; and rule over the fish of the sea and over the birds of the sky and over every living thing that moves on the earth." Then God said, "Behold, I have given you every plant yielding seed that is on the surface of all the earth, and every tree which has fruit yielding seed; it shall be food for you; and to every beast of the earth and to every bird of the sky and to every thing that moves on the earth which has life, I have given every green plant for food"; and it was so. God saw all that He had made, and behold, it was very good. And there was evening and there was morning, the sixth day."
Genesis 1:26-31

In the early descriptions of creation, Genesis says after each phase, God said "And it was good". When God got to the sixth day when man was created, Genesis 1:31 says

God said, "...it was very good". And God rested on the seventh day.

The Trinity had created the perfect world. Then came pride and the fall.

First, it was Lucifer and his band of angels who fell. Lucifer, a created being, thought more highly of himself and thought he was equal to, or even superior to his Creator. Lucifer fell and took a host of angels with him. Filled with pride, Lucifer was determined to arrest control of the world from God and set forth a plan to disrupt all of God's good creation. Sin had entered the world.

The downfall of man started with deception. Lucifer convinced Eve to eat of the tree of knowledge of good and evil. That deception continued on and blinded Adam who also ate the proverbial apple. The result was that man became separated from his Good Father. Man too had fallen.

Lucifer was jumping with glee, he had ruined God's perfect plan for creation, or so he thought. What Lucifer, or Satan, didn't know was that the Creator of the universe already had the perfect plan of restoration and redemption in place. God in His perfect foreknowledge had already conceived the perfect plan for mankind.

Fast forward thousands of years after the atonement phase of God's perfect plan. God was to have His only begotten Son come into the world through a virgin, live a sinless life, die on a cruel cross while taking on Himself our every sin only to rise again on the third day. This is the ultimate plan of restoration that only a perfect God could have conceived.

Here we are today, fallen in sin, prideful, arrogant, self-centered, but *restorable*.

What does this restoration look like? Ultimately, restoration is walking in an upright and sinless life with the perfect, Creator, God Himself. It compares to what Adam and Eve had with God the Father, "walking in the garden in the cool of the day."

The desire of the author is to give you hope that you can also have a sense of restoration with God, Thee Creator, to know that your sins are forgiven, and you can have a joy filled life. This is a Joy that can only be experienced through the restorative work completed on the cross of Calvary.

This is a book of hope that helps you to understand that you too can experience restoration much like characters of old and modern-day people, just like you and me.

In this narrative, you will read about the stories of Old and New Testament Biblical characters who overcame their flaws and sins which kept them from or diminished a pure and holy walk with God Himself. You will also read stories of real life people, in a modern day setting, who overcame their past and now enjoy a rich and rewarding life because of God's forgiveness and restoration. Although their names have all been changed for their protection, it does not, in any way minimize the power of their stories. What matters is simple, they were forgiven and understood how to forgive others and themselves. Most importantly, they now walk in a life of fullness because of the restorative power of the Holy Spirit. Frankly, one of the most significant roles of the Holy Spirit is just that, He restores our communion with Thee Perfect, Holy, Merciful, Gracious, and Loving God.

Receive this encouragement as you take this journey of hope and grace.

Rejected

"Work as unto the Lord. Give it all you've got", they said. "It's for the Kingdom. You know there are blessings in serving God." They said. So they gave it their all.

Joe and Cindy were faithful members and leaders of their local church in Northwestern Louisiana. They had essentially grown up in the church. Not only were they regular attenders, Joe was a Deacon and Cindy was influential on the women's committee.

These two thirty something year olds were the epitome of servanthood. If there was an event going on that needed help, you could always count on Joe and Cindy. They were never afraid of cleaning the bathrooms, mopping floors, cutting the lawn or bringing a dish to a potluck supper. Give it to Joe and Cindy, and it will get done.

As each year passed by, nothing changed. Joe and Cindy had a great life together. While their jobs were nothing special, their main focus was that of raising their children and serving in the church, in that order. Their daughters Sally and Lynette were a handful, but then there was their son, Jonas, he was all boy.

The girls were typical northwestern Louisiana small town girls who loved girl things, playing dress up and playing with their dolls. However, there was the tomboy streak as well. There wasn't anything Jonas, their brother, could do that the girls wouldn't try which included fishing in the river, playing football, bike riding, and so on. These three were in the church almost as often as their parents. In other words, they were a typical family growing up in the 80's and 90's.

One day, Joe came home and said, "There's trouble in River City". The Simmons family was causing problems in church again. This time it was about how they served the Communion. Previously, it was the color of the new carpet the church was replacing during the renovations. What will it be next? Joe said he heard rumblings that there were other issues as well. It was time for another Board Meeting to resolve the latest challenges.

And that was when their lives changed for many years to come. Joe loved sameness and was not fond of change for change sake. Cindy preferred tradition as well but was a little more flexible and could at least look at new ideas, but only if they made sense.

At the church Board Meeting, the Simmons family brought together a coalition of sorts to defend their idea of changing the way they served communion. They wanted change. Not because they needed it, but just to have a change. Everyone listened to their proposal and the traditional sides were drawn. Like Joe and Cindy, there were those who didn't see a need for change. Then there were those who sided with the Simmons' point of view and opinions. To say things got ugly would be a huge understatement. While nothing was physically thrown, there were enough accusations expressed that if there were physical items close by, several people would have gotten hurt by flying objects.

Joe, and several other board members, walked out of the meeting scratching their heads, trying to figure out what just happened. They didn't really talk much about it. The whole thing became quite ridiculous.

A couple of days had gone by without much said by anyone, including Joe and Cindy. In the evening of the third day, Joe received a call from the Board Chairman who asked if he could come by for a short visit. Joe agreed and within minutes, Jack Hastings was ringing his doorbell.

Cindy, in her giftedness, always had some type of dessert for surprise visitors, and Jack was no exception. Joe was at the door in a flash to greet his old friend. "How ya doin' Buddy?" Joe asked Jack, with a very glum look on his face, mumbled, "Not so good. We lost our church." Joe quickly ushered Jack into their living room to sit and talk. What are you talking about, Jack?" Joe snapped. "What in the world do you mean, we lost our church?" Jack replied, "The Simmons group decided that either we would be voted off the board or they would leave. The church is officially splitting. I can't believe it! And over a stupid tray of grape juice. What are we going to do?" Joe asked. "I have no idea. I can't even think straight." Jack responded in disbelief.

They all felt rejected.

And that was the beginning of the end. For the next couple of years, they all tried to sort out the pieces and determine how they would all move forward. These people were friends before, and now some of them wouldn't even talk to each other.

Joe and Cindy's marriage took a turn for the worse as a result of the church split. Their union became cold, dark and just shy of plain existing. Even the smallest things would set off an argument between the two of them. It could be something as simple as what was for dinner or who would pick up the girls from cheer leading practice after school.

As the years past, Joe and Cindy grew farther and farther apart. They still did the usual and routine things together, but the loving spark had dissipated. As the days progressed, Cindy's feeling of rejection intensified. The spark had left their marriage because of a silly little cup of grape juice, but they didn't realize it.

Twenty-five years after the church split, Joe and Cindy had grown numb and were just going through the motions. They were just existing. The numbness came from all the years of Cindy feeling a sense of rejection from her old church and friends. Had she also been rejected by God?

Along came an idea from their daughter, Sally. She met a friend who was raving about this weekend thing. She said it was called Restoration and it helped people with life issues like divorce and death.

Sally couldn't stop talking about it with her friend and decided to "try it out" to see if she would like it.

"Here we go, I'm ready to take a look at this crazy thing." Sally said to her friend, Becky. And off they went. This would be a day of peeling off the layers of hurt and frustrations they both had experienced in their lives. Little did they know how hard it was going to be.

The next day, Sally called her parents and told them about the prior day she and Becky had had. She simply couldn't put their experience into words and insisted that they too go through this crazy thing. After some nudging and pestering, Sally convinced her parents that it would help them get closer to each other and maybe fix some of their issues. Joe and Cindy finally agreed.

The "Restoration" program was happening again in about six weeks. While Joe and Cindy knew they had problems in their marriage, they just couldn't figure out what they were.it was. Time would tell.

The day came that Joe and Cindy too would be "peeling", peeling the layers of hurt off and discovering what was keeping them from having the once loving relationship they used to have.

As the day progressed and the layers were pulled back, Cindy had a huge "Ah ha" moment. It hit her like an anvil crashing down on her. She realized that she had been blaming her church all these years for everything that had happened. Indirectly, Cindy was blaming Joe for their problems and didn't even realize it. She had even been blaming God for all of the strife and the church split.

All of a sudden, Cindy started to wail. The gravity of her new-found truth was almost too much for her to bare. She realized what she had been doing to Joe all these years. She blamed him for losing all her friends, losing her church, and losing her comfort zone. Unknowingly, she had built a wall between herself and everyone else that she had known and loved, isolating herself to avoid being hurt again. Never would she open herself to getting close to anyone; she simply couldn't take that chance.

With this revelation, the wall started to crumble, and the healing had begun. "Restoration" was taking place before everyone's eyes. Now Cindy, herself, started to crumble, shaking and crying out of a sense of grief and remorse at how she had treated Joe. She had lost nearly 25 years of what could have been an amazing married life all due to the wall she had built around herself.

Later that day, all Joe could do was tell everyone that he had gotten his wife back. Her joy had been "restored" right along with their marriage. To look at the two of them, you would think that they were newlyweds.

Amazing things happen when you peel the layers off and get to the core, the truth, of what is keeping you from a thriving relationship with God. In Cindy and Joe's case, it was a matter of her forgiving the leaders of their former church. Cindy realized she had to forgive her husband, even though he had done nothing wrong. She knew she also had to forgive God, who she thought could have prevented everything. All of this was in Cindy's mind and she had to deal with it personally. As she did, she became fully "Restored".

Where else have you seen or experienced an incredible rejection and restoration?

When Paul and Barnabas were sent out on their first mission trip, they were focused and determined to make a difference. They were filled with the Holy Spirit. Along with them on this journey was young, John Mark.

Through a series of events, Mark left Paul and Barnabas when they arrived at Perga in Pamphylia. As a result, Paul developed a bitter taste toward John Mark and he held it against him.

While Acts 13 doesn't tell us the reason why Mark left, Paul held it against him, and to the point that he did not want Mark to travel with him again.

In Acts 15, Paul and Barnabas were planning their second missionary journey. In verse 37, it tells us that Barnabas wanted to take Mark along and give him a second chance; however, Paul insisted that Mark was not reliable and should not be with them. There was such a huge disagreement between the two of them that they separated from each other. Paul chose to take Silas with him and Barnabas took John Mark.

Sometime later, Paul writes in his letter to Timothy, *"Only Luke is with me. Pick up Mark and bring him with you, for he is useful to me for service."*
2 Timothy 4:11.

The restoration had begun. At some point, Paul and John Mark reconciled their differences. In other words, Paul was no longer feeling the rejection of Mark not continuing on from Pamphylia. At the same time, Mark was no longer feeling rejected by Paul regarding not traveling on the second mission trip. It is great to see the restoration between these two and to see that Paul says that John Mark is "useful in service".

Here's a question for you, when someone is rejected, do those who rejected the individual have any responsibility in the restoration process? As believers, should we help in the restoring process, or are we only to be the judge and jury and leave the restoration process up to someone else?

In the case of Paul and Mark, I would suggest that Paul, being the more mature person by matter of age and experience, would have reached out to Mark in order to start the process. On the other hand, since Barnabas was in the mix of things, he might have been the catalyst who facilitated the restoration process.

Either way, what is most important is that restoration obviously had occurred between the two men, and that was the ultimate goal.

Emasculated

Strong, confident, focused, and a selfless leader, these are words that describe Ron after he was restored.

Ron grew up in a typical northeastern home, in an intact family. His maternal grandfather had passed away when he was a young boy, so his parents brought his grandmother, Nana as the grandkids called her, to live with them. For several months, all was good. Ron was excited to have Nana there living with them. He had fond memories of going to see her since he could always stay up late and eat just about anything he wanted to eat. Somewhere along the way, things changed though.

On one particular day, Ron was late coming home from school. He had stopped to play in the park with some school friends and he simply lost track of time. Almost nothing was more fun at the park than to compete on the swing for going the highest without falling out, Ron was no different. Ron was in for the "trophy" and had all the others chanting for him to keep going. No one had ever been as high as he was that day.

All of a sudden, Ron realized how late it was after he heard the chimes from the clock tower nearby. He quickly jumped out of the swing when it was safe and took off in a mad dash to make it home as fast as his legs would take him. Too late, he was already in trouble.

Nana, dear sweet Nana, was there waiting for him with a wooden spoon in her hand. As soon as he crossed the threshold, she started swinging. She didn't even give him a chance to explain why he was late. She just let him have it and sent him to his room wailing.

The severe beating wasn't the worst of it; the verbal abuse soon followed. Ron heard words describing himself that he had never heard before out of his grandmother's mouth. Hurt, shocked and confused, Ron went to his room and cried. After all, what else could a 10-year-old boy do? One of his heroes had just changed right before his eyes and hurt him deeply. What had happened to his sweet grandmother, the one whom he remembered giving him candy and letting him stay up late?

What did he do to deserve this, Ron thought? Yes, he was about an hour late in coming home, but, after all, he was a 10-year-old boy. Boys typically can't tell time that well. Well, actually, boys have boy things on their minds, and time isn't usually one of them.

These occurrences became a pattern for Nana, and if Ron did the slightest thing wrong, he would either get another beating, a verbal put-down, or even both. At least two to three times a week, Ron would get a beating after school and be sent to his room for no reason at all.

Ron tried to talk with his parents on several occasions about what was going on, but they would hear nothing of it. It was almost as if Nana had two different personalities; she would act one way when she was alone with Ron, and another way when there was anyone else within earshot of hearing.

After months of this going on, Ron became a total recluse. The only time he would even acknowledge his Nana was when he was forced to by his parents. She had lied about her behavior, the beatings and verbal abuse. No one believed Ron. As a result, Ron stayed away from everyone.

This negative pattern continued for many years. Although the beatings slowed down, the verbal criticisms seemed to persist and even intensified over time. If Ron received anything less than an A in any of his school subjects, he was called stupid, inept, lazy, a goof off, ignorant, or even an idiot. The names were countless. Sadly, Ron started to believe her, so much so, that his grades started to slip. His A's became B's, then B's became C's. Ron didn't really care. All he wanted to do was pass and get out of the hell hole he was trapped in.

Finally, the day had come when Ron would graduate from high school and he looked forward to moving out and doing whatever he wanted. No more put-downs, no more whacks with a wooden spoon, and no more feelings of worthlessness. He was going to make something of himself.

Through his junior and senior years in high school, he was being recruited by men from the military. They all made it seem like a fantasy - a world where he could get away, travel, see the world, but mainly, get away from his family. Now Ron was faced with the choice of which branch. The hardest part of all of this, he wouldn't be 18 until

August, which meant that he couldn't join without his parent's approval. Unfortunately, they would have nothing to do with it. After all, all the stuff going on in the Middle East was a powder keg and they knew that he would certainly be shipped off there immediately after his basic training.

Soon, Ron took a job with a local construction company doing menial labor. He was the designated hauler and clean up guy. He got everyone their lunch and did the work that no one else wanted to do. While he didn't find much fulfillment in what he was doing, he was saving money and counting the days until he turned 18.

The day before his 18th birthday, he told his boss he would be in late the following day. He had an appointment the following morning with the Marine recruiter and he intended to sign up. That night, Ron could barely sleep due to the anticipation. He couldn't wait to walk into the military office in the morning as a slave to his situation and walk out as a free man, a Marine. That was exactly what he did. What a relief, Ron felt like his life was starting over.

After work that day, Ron walked in the house to make the announcement that in 30 days, he would be leaving for good. He had joined the Marines, and no one could do anything to stop him. The verbal abuse started immediately he told his parents about his new choice of career. From one side, he heard the reprimands from his parents. "We told you not to do this. Why don't you listen to us?" From the other side, he heard words from his grandmother, her words hurt the most. "Boy, they are going to be sorry. They have no idea how lazy you are. You are no good. You will probably get someone else killed. What a fool. You will probably get kicked out within six months. Why in the world would they want you?"

Their words resonated in Ron's head day after day. Had he done the right thing? Would he last the whole four years he signed up for? Ron just couldn't get these things out of his head. He couldn't wait to head off to basic training.

Ron arrived for basic training and was immediately greeted with comments like, "My job is to change you all from being a bunch of babies, into a bunch of proud Marines. You will do what you are told, when you are told. The one word we don't use around here is the word can't. Do you hear me?", the drill sergeant yelled! "I don't care who your mommy or daddy are. From here forward, I'm everything you need. You will ALL become MEN, MARINES! Do you hear me?"

For the first time in years, Ron had hope. He knew he could overcome just about anything. He was finally out of that prison back home and could become something.

Basic training was everything they said it would be. Long days, sleepless nights, running 30 miles with a full load on his back. Then there was weapons training. Ron loved that part of the training. He knew what he wanted to do with his life - to become a weapons expert.

Life was great for the first two years of Ron's Marine career. He loved the routines he faced every day. His friends were exactly that - friends. They all had each other's backs. He could count on every one of them. He knew all the cutting up and put downs they threw at each other were all in jest and in plain fun. These "brothers" all had the utmost respect for each other and would never intentionally do something to hurt one another.

Then it happened, Ron went back home for one of his furloughs just because he didn't have anywhere else to go. One evening he was out with high school friends at a local ice cream shop. Across the room sat "Angel" with a group of girls. Well, that's what she looked like to him anyway. Her real name was Sam, short for Samantha, and she was the center of attention that night. It didn't take long for Ron to get up the courage to interrupt the group who happened to be celebrating Sam's birthday and sharing a 20 scoop ice cream sundae. After all, he was a Marine.

Now Ron was not in his uniform that night, but he always carried himself as any Marine would. With great honor and respect, he introduced himself to Sam. He didn't even notice the other girls sitting around her. Ron quickly complimented her on how pretty she was and called her Angel. "It doesn't really matter what your name is. I think I'll call you Angel because that's what you look like to me", he said confidently to Sam. Blushing, Sam just looked at him, all clean shaven, buzz styled haircut and lean and mean. She stammered a little and replied with a soft spoken, "Thank you, but my name is Samantha, but everyone calls me Sam. What's your name?" Ron quickly replied with, "Ron Jackson, ma'am. I sure would like your phone number. I'm only here for a few more days and would like to get together somewhere. Your call." Sam smiled and said, "Why only a few days, Ron Jackson?" "Well ma'am, I'm on leave from the Marines and I have to report back.", Ron explained.

Very quickly they exchanged phone numbers and they went their separate ways. Sam continued celebrating her birthday and Ron went back to the guys. The giggles didn't stop all night from the girlfriends. "Wow, how did he pick you?" one of the girls said. The next day, Ron picked up the phone and called Sam, as promised. They quickly set a time and place to get together and the rest, as they say, is history.

Later that week, Ron was off to his next assignment. This time, unlike those in the past, he couldn't wait to come back home just so he could spend time with Sam. Their courtship lasted about a year, which was the hardest year of their lives. They would write and occasionally call, but phone lines weren't that great between the US and Kuwait where Ron was stationed for six months.

Ron finally proposed, and they planned their storybook wedding for when Ron was on his next leave. Sam had her hands full with all the wedding plans - dress, cake, bridesmaids, flowers and so on. All Ron had to do was show up looking handsome in his clean, pressed Sergeant's Uniform and sweep her off her feet. Well, maybe not quite that easy, but close.

Ron and Sam had a lovely wedding and became Mr. and Mrs. Jackson. You couldn't find two bigger smiles in the Western hemisphere. Off they went to start their new life together. Who knew what would lie ahead.

After a few years, Ron decided it was time to leave the Marines and stay home. While he loved his life as a Marine, he wanted to be a family man and sleep in his own bed at night instead of a cot in some foreign country. About a year after he retired, he started working for a local police department as the official trainer at their gun range. He taught all the rookie cops how to use their fire arms properly. Ron simply loved it. Not only did he love his work, he loved his family. Yes, family. His relationship with his parents had already been restored, but that's not what he meant by family. Ron and Sam were going to have a baby boy. They could not have been happier. Then came child number two, another boy. Wow, they were proud parents! Everything was going great. Great job, great family, it could not have been any better.

One day, Sam got a call from her mother. It wasn't a good one. Her dad had a very aggressive form of cancer and it looked like he only had six months to a year to live. Her mother asked Sam, "I need help, could you please come home?"

With Sam's mother and father still back in New Jersey and they in Texas, what were they going to do? Ron couldn't just quit his job and leave his career behind. Then there was the promotion he was expecting as well.

For the next several months, Sam lived with her parents half way across the country. The time apart was so difficult for both of them. Ron asked for some time off at work, so he could sort things out. Should he stay where he was and pursue his career, or should he walk away from what he had built to rejoin his wife, children, and in-laws? During this time of separation from Sam, Ron made some very foolish choices that almost cost him his marriage and family. Sadly, he let his pride get in the way.

Ron finally decided to leave his job as the munitions trainer to move back to New Jersey so his whole family could be together. Sadly, a month after Ron moved back, his father-in-law succumbed to the cancer and passed away. During the month, Ron looked tirelessly for a job, something, anything to be able to provide for his family. He could find nothing.

The next few months were nothing but chaos. It seemed that a new pattern started to arise. Ron's mother-in-law had become just like his Nana. She became verbally abusive every day. It was nothing but criticism and belittling. No matter what Ron did, nothing was good enough for her.

Ron decided to move his family back to Texas in hopes to find a good job. Hopefully, he would be able to return to the police force and maybe pick up where he left off. Thirty days later, the truck was packed, and they were on the road. Thankfully, they hadn't sold their house in Texas, so they could just move back in quickly and without much effort. This time though, living at home would be different as Ron's mother-in-law would be living with them. Although he wasn't all too pleased, he knew it was for the best and things would work out.

Nonetheless, the verbal abuse continued from Sam's mother, day after day.

Ron wasn't able to get his old job back, so he resorted to working night security jobs just to pay the bills. "You are a good-for-nothing. You are lazy, a stupid bum. You can't hold down a job. You are nothing but a wretched waste of a man. You don't know how to treat my daughter or my grand babies." Over and over, Ron heard these negative words from his mother-in-law. He fell deeper and deeper into depression. It was his grandmother's words all over again. This time, however, he couldn't escape and asking his mother-in-law to leave would only destroy his wife and kill their marriage.

Ron felt worthless. Again, he didn't feel like much of a man at all. He felt as though he had been emasculated all over again.

Ron started his road to recovery by attending the weekend Restoration program. When he arrived, he sat there with his head low, shoulders forward and feeling worthless, so much so, that he couldn't even make eye contact with anyone in the room.

Throughout the weekend, Ron had the layers of hurt and rejection peeled back. Each hour that passed by, he was revealing more of who he really was. Ron was being restored. He realized that he wasn't all the ugly things he heard from his grandmother and mother-in-law. He wasn't a no good, lazy bum. He had value and he had worth. His worth though, didn't come from the people around him; it didn't come from him being a former Marine or a police officer, Ron's worth came from God.

Ron quickly realized that he was a Mighty Warrior for God, he learned that the enemy was trying to keep him down with depression, emasculation and worthlessness. Ron then knew that he was hearing nothing but a bunch of lies and he wasn't going to listen to them anymore.

Ron had been a follower of Jesus for many years and tried to live a good life. Sadly, because of all the lies he had been listening to over the years, he lost sight of his true strength and worth. Soon after, Ron chose a new life verse to live by. He stood reciting the verse repeatedly, *"I can do ALL things through Him who strengthens ME!"* Philippians 4:13 Over and over, Ron was claiming this verse as his very own. Each time he said it, he got louder and louder. He became a Mighty Warrior for God! Ron had been restored to who he really was in the eyes of God and nothing could hold him down!

As I consider Ron's story, I think about Samson from the Book of Judges. Samson was a mighty warrior for God. Through a series of events, including his own arrogance and pride, he lost all of his strength. He, too, was emasculated. Samson was belittled and ridiculed by his enemies. He was mocked, beaten down, and made fun of by them.

Samson, in his pride, lost everything, including his God-given strength. Likewise, Ron, in his pride, almost lost it all as well.

'It so happened when they were in high spirits, that they said, "Call for Samson, that he may amuse us." So they called for Samson from the prison, and he entertained them. And they made him stand between the pillars. Then Samson said to the boy who was holding his hand, "Let me feel the pillars on which the house rests, that I may lean against them." Now the house was full of men and women, and all the lords of the Philistines were there. And about 3,000 men and women were on the roof looking on while Samson was amusing them. Then Samson called to the Lord and said, "O Lord God, please remember me and please strengthen me just this time, O God, that I may at once be avenged of the Philistines for my two eyes." Samson grasped the two middle pillars on which the house rested, and braced himself against them, the one with his right hand and the other with his left. And Samson said, "Let me die with the Philistines!" And he bent with all his might so that the house fell on the lords and all the people who were in it. So the dead whom he killed

at his death were more than those whom he killed in his life.' Judges 16:25-30

Samson realized his incredible pride-filled mistakes and pleaded with God to give him his strength back one last time in order to avenge the enemies of God, which he should have done in the first place. By grace, God restored his strength one last time to be able to kill all the Philistines. In the process of this act, he once again became a Mighty Warrior for God. He sacrificed everything to bring glory to Almighty God.

While Ron did not need to sacrifice his life in the restoration process, he did have to humble himself and rid himself of his pride.

Today, Ron is living a life of restoration, serving God as a Mighty Warrior.

Shamed

What do you do when someone projects an evil act on you, and you are totally victimized? That is the story of Melvin Kurtz. Melvin was a 45-year-old man who was in the bondage of what someone did to him, 35 years earlier.

Let me take you back to the small, unassuming east Texas cotton and railroad town of Paris, a population of 22,000. Located in the Piney Woods of northeast Texas, its main industry was agriculture and cotton related, but also heavily into healthcare for that region.

Melvin was a typical 10-year-old east Texas boy, growing up in a normal 70's home life. There wasn't much to do in this sleepy railroad and cotton town. However, like all boys that age, he found plenty to get into such as playing baseball, basketball and football, bike riding, not to mention frogs, girls-yuck, and watching the trains. He would imagine what it would be like to jump on board the trains and ride the countryside like a hobo from town to town.

Then there was family. Melvin had an uncle and an aunt. Uncle Tad lived a few blocks away while Aunt Mae lived on the other side of town. It was always great to get together with the entire family, including his four cousins. When the cousins were all together, they would always find trouble to get into. They had great imaginations as Melvin would say.

While he enjoyed spending time with Aunt Mae, she wasn't his favorite. She was his mom's sister, and that meant, his mom knew everything he did. Funny thing, it was almost as if he had a second mom at times. "Melvin, go wash your hands. Melvin, did you eat your vegetables? Melvin, stop running in the house" That was all Melvin heard.

Then there was Uncle Tad. He was always living on the edge. He always had fun things to do. Some of it, Melvin didn't even understand, but he would always be able to entertain the family. Uncle Tad used to say that Melvin was his favorite of all his nieces and nephews.

Uncle Tad was originally got married years ago, but his wife left him about six years ago. Ron didn't really know why, but one day she was gone. No one talked about it either. Uncle Tad had a lot of lady friends coming by to visit and had some men friends that came by from time to time as well.

One hot summer day, Melvin was bored with nothing to do and no one to do it with. His mom and dad were both off working so he was all alone. Uncle Tad stopped by to borrow a tool from Buster, that is what they called Melvin's dad. Buster wasn't home at the time to give it to him, and that was when Melvin's life changed in a horrible way.

Uncle Tad told Melvin he wanted to show him something inside the house. Before he knew it, Melvin found himself alone in his bedroom, in a very strange situation with his uncle. First, there were odd comments from Uncle Tad like, "When do you want to become a man? Do you trust me? Do you love your parents? You wouldn't want anything to happen to your parents, would you?" The next thing he knew, Uncle Tad had him taking his clothes off as he too stripped down to nothing. Twenty minutes later, Uncle Tad got dressed and started to leave the house. On his way out of the house he said, "Melvin, this is our little secret. You wouldn't want anything to happen to your parents now, would you?"

For the remainder of the summer, this was the pattern. Every time Uncle Tad went by the house, if Melvin was there, they ended up the same way. Fall came, and the pattern continued, but now it was just after school. Melvin became so confused and afraid. He really liked his uncle but didn't like what he was doing. At the same time, Melvin was afraid that something would happen to one of his parents, if they found out what was going on. He couldn't tell anyone.

Melvin felt all alone and trapped in whatever this was. He went from being a fun loving ten-year-old boy, to a loner. He used to laugh a lot but not so much anymore. He forced himself to laugh until his uncle came around. Then Melvin just avoided his uncle completely.

No matter what Melvin said, his uncle seemed to have some kind of spell over him. Melvin knew what was going on was wrong, but he simply couldn't stop his uncle for fear of what the consequences would be. Melvin felt very alone!

This went on for well over two years and over the course of time, Melvin started losing weight. He didn't want to eat much and seemed to be depressed most of the time.

25

His parents even took him to the doctor to see if they could figure out what was wrong, but the doctor was just as baffled as his parents.

Finally, it stopped. One day, Melvin's father came home from work early to tell him that his uncle was very sick with cancer and wouldn't be around very long. This threw Melvin into an even greater tailspin. At 12, Melvin thought he caused the cancer somehow. The guilt was overwhelming Melvin more and more each day. While suicide never really crossed his mind, he had thought seriously about running away and simply getting lost, and maybe on one of those southbound trains that came through town. Lost, alone, confused, ashamed, that was who Melvin Kurtz had become.

Uncle Tad passed away about six months later. Melvin didn't really know how to react. Should he be happy or sad? He just stayed confused and became even more of a quiet loner.

Melvin picked up the pieces as best he could and continued on through his school years right into High School. His least favorite subject was Physical Education. He hated taking showers with the other guys as it prompted flashbacks to times with his Uncle Tad. It made him sick all over again. Melvin tried everything to get out of PE class but without any success.

Melvin finally finished high school and was ready to get on with life. He found a job in an auto parts store. He seemed to favor fast things like cars and motorcycles, especially the Mustangs and Camaros. While he couldn't afford either on his small salary, he would often go to the outskirts of town to watch the guys race their cars.

Melvin made a lot of friends out there, and it was fun just being around the guys. One day, Melvin met Robby. He was about 11 years old and he too loved fast cars. Over the coming weeks, Melvin saw Robby there several times and always made sure he went to talk with him.

Then it happened. Melvin suggested to Robby that he had something he wanted to show him, but behind an abandoned gas station. The ugly, vicious cycle had begun. Melvin had flashbacks of what his uncle had done to him and simply could not control himself. It had become obvious that Melvin's brain had been programed to a behavior that was not normal as a result of what his uncle had done to him.

Melvin had become the grown up that was suggesting things to Robby about loving his parents, not wanting anything bad to happen to them...etc. He too warned Robby to keep this between the two of them. This destructive behavior continued for several weeks. Melvin would go to the car races and lure Robby behind the gas station. Melvin had become the molester, not the molested.

After a few weeks, Robby asked his parents some questions about the "birds and the bees". Where did that come from, they wondered. After asking a few questions of their own, they became very curious and concerned. One Friday night, Robby's parents followed him and his friends out to the make-shift race track. They kept out of sight so Robby wouldn't know they were there. In shock, they watched as Melvin took Robby back behind the gas station one last time. That was that. Robby's dad was so incensed and furious while he followed his son and Melvin to the secret place. It took every bit of strength to keep him from killing Melvin. Robby's mom asked someone to call the police who arrived in a flash. Next thing he knew, Melvin had handcuffs on and was being taken to the Paris Police station. Melvin had been caught in the act.

It wasn't long before Melvin was in the courtroom on charges of child molestation. The evidence was cut and dry. In only three days, his life changed forever. He was found guilty, convicted and sentenced to 20 years in prison. But what about his shame?

For nearly ten years, Melvin lived in the shame of what his uncle had done to him. His own shame drove him to become the perpetrator. He just wasn't thinking normally. Uncle Tad, even though he was dead and gone, was still controlling Melvin's thoughts and behavior.

Fast forward, Melvin did his time, paid his debt to society and was released from being behind the physical prison bars; however, he wasn't "free" from his emotional captivity.

Now at 45, Melvin was living with the shame of being a sexual predator. He would forever have to carry that degrading label which negatively impacted the kinds of jobs he held, where he lived, and even who he could be around.

Thankfully, he found himself in the Restoration program. Very quickly, Melvin revealed his past and admitted that he needed help. The emotional layers were pulled back and the ugliness of his past was out in the open. He had paid the punishment for his crimes against Robby, but he was still riddled and held captive with shame. Melvin finally realized that what he was carrying was shame from what someone did to him. After all, he was an innocent young boy, only 10 years old at the time. How could he possibly understand the magnitude of what was going on? Plus, he had to protect his parents. He feared for their safety.

Guilt and shame are very close cousins when it comes to Satan's deceptive tricks and lies. Melvin initially thought he was guilty for what his Uncle Tad had done to him. After going through a restorative exercise, it became clear to him that he wasn't at fault for what happened to him as a young boy. Even at the age of 45, Melvin was finally able to rid himself of the shame he had been carrying for nearly 30 years. He was being restored to the life he knew before he turned ten. He could finally look himself in the mirror and not feel totally disgusted. He didn't have to wear the moniker of shame any more.

How many other people are just like Melvin? Millions are carrying what they think is guilt, which in reality is the shame others put on them. In the Bible, there's a story of a woman who was a harlot. She lived a very sinful life. Was this her choice or was she forced into the lifestyle? No matter what her choices were, she was filled with guilt and shame. She realized that the only way she could rid herself of the shame was to go to the One who could forgive her sins.

"Now one of the Pharisees was requesting Him to dine with him, and He entered the Pharisee's house and reclined at the table. And there was a woman in the city who was a sinner; and when she learned that He was reclining at the table in the Pharisee's house, she brought an alabaster vial of perfume, and standing behind Him at His feet, weeping, she began to wet His feet with her tears, and kept wiping them with the hair of her head, and kissing His feet and anointing them with the perfume. Now when the Pharisee who had invited Him saw this, he said to himself, "If this man were a prophet He would know who and what sort of person this woman is who is touching Him, that she is a sinner." And Jesus answered him, "Simon, I have something to say to you." And he replied, "Say it, Teacher." "A moneylender had two debtors: one owed five hundred denarii, and the other fifty. When they

were unable to repay, he graciously forgave them both. So which of them will love him more?" Simon answered and said, "I suppose the one whom he forgave more." And He said to him, "You have judged correctly." Turning toward the woman, He said to Simon, "Do you see this woman? I entered your house; you gave Me no water for My feet, but she has wet My feet with her tears and wiped them with her hair. You gave Me no kiss; but she, since the time I came in, has not ceased to kiss My feet. You did not anoint My head with oil, but she anointed My feet with perfume. For this reason, I say to you, her sins, which are many, have been forgiven, for she loved much; but he who is forgiven little, loves little." Then He said to her, "Your sins have been forgiven." Those who were reclining at the table with Him began to say to themselves, "Who is this man who even forgives sins?" And He said to the woman, "Your faith has saved you; go in peace." Luke 7:36-50

The question for you is -are you carrying guilt or shame? There is only one way to completely rid yourself of either of these, and to be fully restored and renewed. You must confess your sins, repent, and ask God to forgive you of your sins. No sin is too great or small for God.

Melvin confessed, repented, and sought forgiveness for his ways. His shame was gone. He was restored.

 Tempted

Ann Brooks was one of the most unassuming ladies around. She was sweet, thoughtful and always looking out for the other person. That was why it was so shocking to discover her deep dark secret.

Ann's husband, George, was a significant figure in the oilfield in West Texas. He hadn't always been there as he used to float, so to speak, from one offshore rig to another. He finally made it his home, Monday through Thursday at least, in the Permian Basin in West Texas. It was hot in the summer and cold in the winter. All that you could see for miles around was dirt, tumble weeds and little scrub trees, oh and oil derricks. Not exactly your land of paradise. About the only thing going for it was the oil, at least that was what George would say.

Back to Ann. For over 20 years, Ann had lived the life of a "weekend wife". When George left on Monday mornings, she knew she had a lot of free time throughout the week. Once her work was done around the house, it was her time to do whatever she chose. George's income was sufficient for them, so she didn't need to hold down a job of any sort. Ann tried working a part time retail job for a few months, but she felt confined, she needed to be out in the open air as much as she thought was possible.

Ann was totally bored on this particular spring day, so she went into a local restaurant with a lounge in the back. She ordered a quick sandwich but then decided she would get an adult beverage to start her afternoon. She found herself ordering another drink and just sat there for a couple of hours. This became her watering hole for the next several months.

One day while at the restaurant just pondering life, Bill stopped by for a little chat. He had noticed her there for a few weeks and wanted to get her story. Ann kindly invited Bill to join her and the conversation took off. Ann wasn't looking for a new companion of any sort as she was totally content with her husband and marriage.

This became somewhat of a regular thing - Ann and Bill just sitting there visiting for an hour or two at a time. Then one day, Bill asked Ann a rather peculiar question. He asked, "You drink a margarita or two almost every day. Have you ever considered anything a little stronger?" Ann responded, "What do you have in mind?". "Well, it isn't a drink, but I promise you will like it." Bill replied.

That afternoon, Bill invited Ann to join him at his apartment and promised that he would give her something good. Without hesitation, Ann agreed to join him. Little did she know then, she would develop a 20-year addiction to cocaine.

First, it was just a little something for recreational purposes. Then it grew each week with the need getting greater with every line. Before she knew it, she was hooked on a $75 a day drug habit. George wasn't aware of the financial impact, as he gave her a wad of cash each weekend and she could spend it any way she wanted to.

This soon became Ann's routine. As soon as George left town on Monday morning, Ann met with Bill to get her weekly supply, then on Thursday, Ann would take her last line and clean up just in time before George returned home. This pattern continued for almost 20 years. Day after day, week after week, month after month, and year after year. As a result, Ann had become an addict and she didn't even realize it. She became so dependent on cocaine that she could barely function without it. Sometimes, the weekends were brutal. If she went more than her normal three days without her drugs, she would become so irritable.

For years she was able to hide it from her husband, or so she thought. While George never said anything, he suspected something was going on. While their relationship was reasonably good, there were minor issues that would come up from time to time. Nothing, however, that would jeopardize the good thing she had going.

One day, Ann had decided that she was going to try to kick the habit and went a week without a fix. She ran into Janet, one of her friends, at the mall and started visiting her. Ann became so disoriented at some point that she was talking in irrational sentences. Janet got concerned and worried. A few days later, Janet stopped by her house for a visit and to check up on Ann. Ann revealed that she was miserable and hated her life, she hated George traveling all the time and being along from Monday till Thursday night.

She simply didn't like who she had become. And that was just what Janet needed to hear.

"Ann," Janet said, "I have a program I want you to go to that will help with all your anxiety and depression. I went through the program a while back and I feel like a different person. I really think you will like it." Ann immediately started to talk defensively, "I don't need anything. I'm fine." After a few minutes, Janet had convinced Ann to at least think about the program.

Within a few days, Ann had hit rock bottom and called Janet asking, "What's the name of that program?" Janet quickly replied, "It's called Restoration, and that is exactly what you will get." "OK." Ann responded. "I'll go, what could it hurt?"

Ann registered for the program a few days later and had psyched herself up. The day had come, and she was off to her time of renewal. Little did she know the radical change she was about to experience.

She arrived at the meeting place not knowing a single person. She felt like a duck out of water. As Ann looked around the room, she thought to herself, "What the heck am I doing here? I don't need this. This is just stupid." As the evening progressed, she .warmed up to others that were there in the group with her. "Well, I guess they aren't so bad," she thought.

As the hours progressed and everyone was opening up, peeling away their individual layers and revealing what they had underneath their personal "onions". Many had started their healing process, but for Ann, not so much.

Towards the end of the second day, Ann, still stoic, had little positive movement in healing. She was being as stubborn as a mule. She did not want to let go or open up. She was so riddled with the fear of what other people would think of her, she simply couldn't start the healing process.

Then all of a sudden, Ann was put on the "hot seat" and confronted with her own personal reality. She was asked a very pointed question. "If you leave here today, what will have changed? Will you have peace in your life? Will you continue to live in fear? How long will you last based on the course you have chosen?

Immediately, Ann broke down and confessed her 20-year addiction. She admitted that she was terrified of walking out the doors and being all alone. She said she couldn't live without her drugs and certainly not by herself at least.

She was then asked a simple question. "Ann, what if you didn't have to do it alone? What if you had someone to come along beside you and walk the walk with you?" With that, one person after another came along beside her and said, "I'll be there." "I'll be there." "I'll be there for you, Ann." "Ann, you can count on me." When it was all finished, 31 people within this group who were once strangers, stood by Ann, committing to be there for her.

She had been totally restored. She had broken the habit. The chains of drug addiction were ripped apart. Ann was finally free of her addiction. Better yet, she was not even the least bit tempted to indulge again.

On the following Monday, George left for work as usual to head to west Texas. There was one major change after he left this time. By one o'clock, Ann's phone had rung 13 times. One by one, her new friends from Restoration, called to encourage her. Each one that called told her over and over, "I'm here for you. If you need me to come over, I'll be right there." By eight o'clock that night, 27 people had called or texted Ann. She had beaten the first day. She had broken the chains., she truly felt restored.

Through God's Grace, all temptation for Ann was gone. Her new friends stepped in and were there for her. Ann had a glow of peace that overwhelmed her. Restoration felt so good!

When you have everything, temptation comes in different forms. What if you could have any woman, or man, in your kingdom at your beck and call? If you saw something you liked, just go for it. That was the case with King David. If he wanted something, he just told one of his servants to get it for him and there it was.

One day, David was on one of his many balconies in his enormous palace when he happened to look across the way and saw Bathsheba bathing on her rooftop. "Wow, she is beautiful." He said to himself. "I want that!" One of his servants overheard the king and inquired, "Master, shall I get her for you?" King David was so tempted and decided, why not, I'm the king. I can have anything I want. The servant quickly went and got Bathsheba and brought her to his highness. David and Bathsheba had relations and as a result, she became pregnant.

Not long after they found out that she was pregnant, David had her husband killed by sending him to the front battle lines. Here, David was confronted by his friend Nathan.

"Then the LORD sent Nathan to David. And he came to him and said, "There were two men in one city, the one rich and the other poor. "The rich man had a great many flocks and herds. "But the poor man had nothing except one little ewe lamb which he bought and nourished; And it grew up together with him and his children. It would eat of his bread and drink of his cup and lie in his bosom, and was like a daughter to him. "Now a traveler came to the rich man, and he was unwilling to take from his own flock or his own herd, to prepare for the wayfarer who had come to him;

Rather he took the poor man's ewe lamb and prepared it for the man who had come to him." Then David's anger burned greatly against the man, and he said to Nathan, "As the LORD lives, surely the man who has done this deserves to die. He must make restitution for the lamb fourfold, because he did this thing and had no compassion." Nathan then said to David, "You are the man! Thus, says the LORD God of Israel, 'It is I who anointed you king over Israel and it is I who delivered you from the hand of Saul. I also gave you your master's house and your master's wives into your care, and I gave you the house of Israel and Judah; and if that had been too little, I would have added to you many more things like these! Why have you despised the word of the LORD by doing evil in His sight? You have struck down Uriah the Hittite with the sword, have taken his wife to be your wife, and have killed him with the sword of the sons of Ammon. Now therefore, the sword shall never depart from your house, because you have despised Me and have taken the wife of Uriah the Hittite to be your wife.' Thus says the LORD, 'Behold, I will raise up evil against you from your own household; I will even take your wives before your eyes and give them to your companion, and he will lie with your wives in broad daylight. Indeed you did it secretly, but I will do this thing before all Israel, and under the *sun.'" Then David said to Nathan, "I have sinned against the LORD." And Nathan said to David, "The LORD also has taken away your sin; you shall not die. However, because by this deed you have given occasion to the enemies of the LORD to blaspheme, the child also that is born to you shall surely die." So Nathan went to his house. Then the LORD struck the child that Uriah's widow bore to David, so that he was very sick."*

2 Samuel 12:1-15

David's temptation overtook him, and he paid the price for it. There were many problems that came up in his kingdom and in his family as a result of what he did.

An odd thing happened though, David was restored. While he had to deal with his own guilt and shame, God granted him favor. In fact, it was some time after the events that God said David was a man after His own heart. Even with his sin, he was restored. That is what I call full restoration.

For 20 years, Ann succumbed to the temptations of her cocaine habits. Her temptation was too strong for her to deal with alone. While she did not have anyone killed, she was still in mental bondage, much like King David.

Ann realized she was incapable of traveling this road alone. Friends literally lined up to support her in her time of need much like Nathan stood by David.

Ann had been restored, and her tendencies to fall into temptation had been taken away. Ann was no longer in bondage to her drugs.

Objectified

Growing up in a typical small town in the central part of Texas, Candy led a charmed life for her first 11 years. Her real name was Catherine, but everyone called her Candy. She did all the typical 11-year-old girl things you would expect, like playing dress up with girlfriends, skating parties, and cheerleading for the teams.

While life was somewhat typical, she dealt with the confusions of family life in a blended family. Candy had a natural sister, age 9 and a step brother, age 16. Her mother divorced her father when she was seven and remarried three years later. Her new step father was a hard worker at the feed mill on the out skirts of town. For most of the year his working hours were pretty normal, from eight to five o'clock, and when fall came around, it was six in the morning until nine or ten o'clock at night. The only days he had off were those days when it rained.

Candy's mother was a part-time nurse at the local nursing home and generally worked the late afternoon or evening shift. Candy was usually just getting home from school when her mom was leaving for work.

Albert, or Al for short, was Candy's new big brother. At 16, he knew everything. He became a big shot at school after he received his driver's license. She always looked up to him and liked following him around like a little puppy. Candy especially liked all the attention she got from Al's friends.

At first, life was good with her new stepfather and older brother, but things took a dramatic change two years later. Candy's stepfather was getting frustrated with life in general and started drinking after work. Often times he would simply come home after work and pass out in his recliner. He didn't talk much and thankfully slept through the evening, so he had no clue what was going on in and around the house.

Life for Candy was just a little dysfunctional and she tried entertaining herself as much as she could. Since they lived a little out of town, the self-produced entertainment was somewhat challenging at times. If Al was around, she could at least pester him like any little sister would. Frequently though, he was off in his 12-year-old Mustang, showing everyone just how cool he was.

One Thursday afternoon, Al's friend Bubba came by looking for him, but he was out running around in his classy Mustang. Candy remembers the exact day and time Bubba came by because it changed her life forever. Since Al wasn't home, Bubba asked if he could stay and wait for him to return. He was one of the cool jocks at school. While Bubba was on the football team, he wasn't very good, so he didn't get to play much. Regardless, he was still pretty strong and in good shape.

Out behind the house was a barn that the family used mainly for storage, but Al and his dad would work on old cars as well. The latest project was a brown and rust colored

1962 Chevy Corvair. They were so determined to get it working and road worthy. While waiting on the front porch with Bubba, he asked Candy if she would take him around to the garage to look at the car and see the progress Al and his dad were making.

Candy thought Bubba was kind of cute, especially because he was paying attention to her, and this made her feel a little older than what she actually was. As they walked to the barn, Bubba started joking around with Candy, punching each other on the arm as a brother and sister would do. It became somewhat of a challenge to see how hard each other would hit. Bubba, of course, was holding back. They finally came to the Corvair, and as they leaned over to look in the car, Bubba posed a question to Candy. "Have you ever been kissed by a man?" A bit surprised and embarrassed, she immediately responded by saying, "Only my father and stepdad." Bubba laughed. "You know what I mean.", as he gave her a one-eyed wink. "I don't know any other men." She quickly responded. With a little chuckle, Bubba moved toward Candy in an attempt to kiss her. While she initially pushed him away, it wasn't a full-blown shove, and in a short while, she was in a full embrace with her 18-year-old friend and didn't quite know what to do next.

For the next few weeks, Bubba would come by the house pretending to look for Al, but in reality, he was looking for Candy.

One day while back in the barn, Bubba asked a strange question. Knowing that Candy liked all kinds of sports, he asked her if she liked baseball. "Of course," she responded.

"Well, let me show you another version." In little or no time, they were sitting in the back seat of the Corvair and Bubba's hands were all over her, trying to take off her shirt.

Stunned and afraid, Candy, wasn't quite sure what to do. Should she scream? Would anyone hear her? Should she fight? Bubba was easily 75 pounds heavier than Candy and a lot stronger. Bubba told her not to fight it; she would like it. Then he reminded her that he was a "big man" in school.

In a flash, the encounter was over. Candy sat there in the back of the car in complete shock. She simply didn't know quite what to do next or what to say. Should she tell her stepfather or stepbrother? Should she tell her mother? These questions ran through her mind with no reasonable answer to any of them. Candy felt all alone.

The pattern continued for months. Sometimes Bubba would bribe her for secrecy. As the trend of events progressed, Bubba introduced Candy to alcohol which seemed to help keep the code of silence. It also helped Candy forget. One day, when she tried to push him away, Bubba pulled out some drugs knowing they would do the trick and make her comply.

Before long, Candy was hooked on the drugs. Soon, she found herself hooked on both the drugs and sex, and she couldn't get enough of either of them. Candy couldn't wait for her daily fix of both. This became a routine for her. Often times, Bubba would pick her up from school to continue their escapade. There were days when Bubba would bring along a friend who would initially be a lookout. As time went on, these "friends" would have their way with Candy as well.

Now at 14, Candy was totally hooked on every kind of drug and as much sex as you could imagine. Bubba soon started arranging encounters with Candy. For every person who would pay, he got a cut of the action. Bubba became Candy's pimp. As long as Bubba gave her drugs, she was compliant. Any time she objected, Bubba threatened to either take her drugs away, or tell her parents.

Shortly after she turned 15, Bubba convinced her to go away with him for a weekend to the city. He said that there were some exciting things going on there. What Candy didn't know was that Bubba had connected with a real pimp who was looking for some new girls. He had just sold Candy and imprisoned her in a world that would take her years to break out of.

In eight years, Candy had become a full-fledged prostitute, traveling to all the major cities, being traded from one pimp to another. Whenever she started to become too comfortable with her surroundings, she moved. It was easy for the pimps to move her since she was totally reliant on drugs and they knew she couldn't live without them.

With each new city came starting over again. That meant going to clubs, dancing, and building her next client base. Now at 22, Candy was hooked even more on drugs, sex and alcohol. Day after day, she knew the routine. She also knew that if she didn't comply, she would lose her drugs, alcohol, sex, and probably get a beating. On several occasions, Candy would have too much to drink and find herself in the back of a police car, on her way to the precinct to sober up. She would then be let out a day or two later and the cycle would start all over again. When would it end?

One day, one of the vice officers recognized her and set a plan in motion to help her escape the abhorrent lifestyle. What Candy didn't know was that Tom was involved with a group of "rescuers" at his church. They called themselves the "ROWers". The official name of the group was Rescuers of Women. And their mission was to help women enslaved to this lifestyle.

Candy became the "project" of Stacy and Janice who were also rescued and restored from much of the same lifestyle earlier in their lives. They were now dedicated as "ROWers" to help young women. For the next few months, they were there for Candy. They found out where Candy lived and would show up often. Sometimes they came with food, clean clothes, or just to talk. Their message was the same - "Jesus loves you, wants to save you, and take you out of this lifestyle."

Initially the visits were once a week, then twice a week, then every other day. Each time they visited her, they had two or three male companions close by. These men had two purposes for being there - for protection and example. Protection was an obvious reason. Candy lived in unusually rough neighborhoods which were not at all safe for Stacy and Janice to be alone.

As an example, Tom and the other men all knew how to treat women with the honor and respect they deserved. Candy witnessed each time what it was like to be truly cared for with total dignity.

One day, Candy broke down and asked Janice and Stacy for sincere help. She wanted to leave this lifestyle but didn't know where to start or where to go. Both ladies knew the formula that helped dozens of other women and they made all the arrangements to take Candy to a halfway house. This wasn't just a halfway house, it also had a "clean-up" facility attached. By this time, Candy had been hooked on drugs, alcohol, and sex for over ten years and they knew she would need some serious detox.

For the next several months, Candy experienced some of the most intense pain, mental, physical, and emotional, that she ever felt in her life. She was soon reunited with her mother and stepfather for short visits after she had no contact with them for over five years. They simply had no clue where she was most of the time.

What Candy didn't know was, that the most significant component of this rescue program was prayer. Yes, prayer. There was a team of "ROWers" that were prayer warriors for these halfway house girls, and their prayers were being answered all the time.

During one particular visit, Stacy, Janice, and Tom shared more of why they initially reached out to Candy. Their mission was not just to help rescue women, but to give them a life of freedom in Christ. Candy had heard the Gospel shared many times but today seemed different. She was finally rid of all the drugs in her system and could think clearly. As they shared the Gospel, she finally understood and felt the love of Christ for the first time in her life. While she felt her burdens being lifted, she still felt like she was in bondage. Tom, Stacy, and Janice all knew she was ready for the next step of restoration in their plan.

Stacy made all the arrangements for Candy to go through the Restoration program in three weeks. She even agreed to take her and spend the weekend close by, just in case it was too overwhelming.

The day had come, Candy and Stacy took off mid-morning to ensure they arrived at the program on time. It was about a four-hour drive and Stacy wanted Candy to be well rested for the intense weekend. As Stacy dropped Candy off, they shared a huge hug and Stacy gave her one last bit of encouragement, "Fight through this. Fight for yourself and for your freedom."

When Stacy arrived back at a friend's house, they had already set a plan in place. The plan was simple, gather a group of friends together and pray for Candy around the clock. These new, unknown friends all had two-hour schedules assigned. For the next two days, someone would be interceding for Candy every minute of the hour, of the day.

Candy was carrying so much hurt, pain, and rejection and she needed a lot of prayers. Being a victim of this abuse for so many years, she had buried memories very far deeper than she imagined. The program facilitators had their work cut out for them. Layer by layer, she managed to reveal her own ugliness to everyone. She wanted to run away so badly, but she promised Stacy she would fight for her freedom. Then she remembered she had put Bubba so far out of her mind it was almost as if he didn't even exist anymore. She now knew exactly what she needed to do to break free, she needed to forgive Bubba for getting her trapped in that lifestyle.

Candy stood in front of her peers and fought for her freedom and restoration. Initially, it was difficult to remember all the details, but she knew she had to recall them in order to be set free. One by one, Candy stated the offense and forgave Bubba stating, "Bubba, I forgive you for…" Each time, you could see her countenance change. If you were there, you would sense her being restored to a whole person once again. Candy broke down and sobbed uncontrollably. This time was different, she was finally able to release all the anger and bitterness she had carried for the past ten years.

Candy was set free. She did it. She fought for herself as Stacy encouraged her to do and got her well-deserved freedom. The tears changed from anger and bitterness; to release; to freedom, and then joy. Candy had been restored! She was no longer someone else's object. She became God's princess.

"The king said, "Is there not yet anyone of the house of Saul to whom I may show the kindness of God?" And Ziba said to the king, "There is still a son of Jonathan who is crippled in both feet." So the king said to him, "Where is he?" And Ziba said to the king, "Behold, he is in the house of Machir the son of Ammiel in Lo-debar." Then King David sent and brought him from the house of Machir the son of Ammiel, from Lo-debar. Mephibosheth, the son of Jonathan the son of Saul, came to David and fell on his face and prostrated himself. And David said, "Mephibosheth." And he said, "Here is your servant!" David said to him, "Do not fear, for I will surely show kindness to you for the sake of your father Jonathan, and will restore to you all the land of your grandfather Saul; and you shall eat at my table regularly." Again, he prostrated himself and said, "What is your servant, that you should regard a dead dog like me?" Then the king called Saul's servant Ziba and said to him, "All that belonged to Saul and to all his house I have given to your master's grandson. You and your sons and your servants shall cultivate the land for him, and you shall bring in the produce so that your master's grandson may have food; nevertheless Mephibosheth your master's grandson shall eat at my table regularly." Now Ziba had fifteen sons and twenty servants. Then Ziba said to the king, "According to all

that my lord the king commands his servant so your servant will do." So Mephibosheth ate at David's table as one of the king's sons.
2 Samuel 9:3-11

Candy had lost all hope of living a normal life. She lost her family and friends as she became the object of other people's pleasures. She felt totally trapped.

While Mephibosheth had grown up in a totally different lifestyle, he too now felt trapped as he lost all of his family's wealth. David showed mercy and brought him back into the royal palace. Again, he felt like royalty.

For the first time in a very long time, Candy felt like royalty, a princess.

Runner

A runner is someone who either can't or won't deal with an issue, so they either sweep it under the carpet or they try to run and hide, hoping things just go away. When they are finally forced to deal with challenges, they often explode and hurt a lot of people in the process.

Along comes Billy, a confident good-looking young man, about 28 years of age who was married to a cute gal. Life looked good in the long term for him, but there was only one problem though, Billy had a major anger issue. On the outside, you would think he had it all together. Billy was cool, confident, and for the most part, easy-going with a unique sense of humor, that was until someone hit a trigger. Sadly, people were hitting his triggers more and more frequently. Some were big triggers, some small, but it didn't really matter. Billy either exploded or he ran, depending on the situation.

Billy grew up in a broken home. His mom and dad divorced when he was about 10 years old. Shortly after his parent's divorce, his dad moved to another town, four hours away. This was when the foundation of Billy's anger problems was laid.

Initially, things were tough. Billy's mom, Heather had only worked little jobs that didn't pay much as she didn't really have any marketable skill. She learned quickly that she needed to go back to school to further her education. Very soon, Heather landed an office managerial position at a small dental clinic, and everything went well. Unfortunately, Heather was either not around in the evenings or she focused on her own school homework, so she didn't spend a lot of time with Billy or his sister. The only time the two of them weren't fighting was when they were asleep. Sadly, the patterns were set in stone for him; he was angry all the time.

A short time after Heather started back to school, she realized she needed help. A brilliant thought came to her mind, to get her mom, or Mom-Mom as the grandkids called her, to move in and help out. What a great idea that was! Mom-Mom loved the grandkids, and they loved her. It was always fun to visit her as they got to stay up late, play games, and eat all the junk food they could find. You know, the typical grandmother to grandchild relationship.

The day had come when Mom-Mom would move in. It was going to be fun all the time, or so they thought.

Something strange happened, Mom-Mom changed the day after she moved in. She was no longer fun to be with and was all about chores and homework. No music, no TV, no friends, except on weekends. From where did this female ogre appear, they thought? What happened to their Mom-Mom? As a result, the anger problem Billy had worsened. Now he was arguing with his sister and his grandmother all the time. Heather tried to be the peacemaker, but that was difficult with her school and work schedule. After a while, they all just stopped talking with each other. While this went on for several years, Heather was hopeful that something would change.

Let's fast forward a little. Billy struggled with a lot of pent up anger and bitterness. While he was an overall terrific guy, his anger came out at some of the most inopportune times. When he was just over 18 years old, he had taken as much as he could. It was time to move out, and that he did. Billy's Mom-Mom had pushed him too far and he was tired of the constant badgering and telling him he would never amount to anything.

It wasn't long before Billy and a couple of buddies rented a small, three-bedroom house together. All was great, until Grace came into his life. Her parents named her well. Even with Billy's anger fits, she showed him grace.

A couple of years after they met, they got married. While the first six months of marriage were great, Billy's anger triggers became greater and more frequent. He soon settled into a new way of dealing with his anger and uncomfortable situations by either shutting down or running away. Billy became an expert at sweeping things under the rug instead of dealing with them. As a result, the anger and resentment grew like wildfire, and got out of control. Life was no longer very pretty for them.

The money they were making was not sufficient to meet their basic needs, so Billy and Grace, decided to move in with Heather. There was plenty of room as Mom-Mom had moved out a few months earlier. For a few months, Billy got control over his temper, but it still flared up from time to time.

Without warning, Heather hit one of her son's triggers and a tornado went swirling through the house. Heather would have nothing of Billy's anger rages and gave him an ultimatum, to either get help or move out. Sadly, Grace found herself right in the middle, not knowing which side to take. She tried to keep peace, but each day became more difficult than the previous.

Heather was talking with a friend, Kathy, one day about her situation with Billy as she was at the end of her rope. Kathy had shared a personal experience she had with a program called Restoration. She described how after her divorce she was always angry and bitter, and how this had crept into other facets of her life. Restoration helped her deal with her issues in ways she never thought possible.

Heather, now armed with a solution, suggested that Billy and Grace go through the program. While he thought it was silly, Grace had a different opinion and wanted to go. Sadly, Billy dug in his heals and refused to go. Heather had a great idea and suggested that she would go to check things out first, and that's exactly what she did. Something funny happened, Heather realized that she was still carrying a lot of bitterness toward her ex-husband and was projecting some of it onto Billy without even realizing it. After that weekend, she changed and began treating Billy with a lot more respect and honor.

This went on for a few months and Billy was amazed by the remarkable change in his mom. Because he was able to witness this change before his own eyes, he softened towards the idea of attending the program which would be offered again in just a few weeks' time. Billy finally agreed to go with Grace.

Early in the Restoration weekend, Billy was doing fine, but as the program went on, he started to peel away the layers that had been built over the years, and his anger toward his grandmother came to the surface. With each layer peeled back, Billy was tempted to run away, and a couple of times he actually did, refusing to finish the program. Somehow, the program directors and his small group counselor managed to encourage him to return to the session and continue working on his anger.

Billy's "ah-ha" moment came when he realized that he needed to forgive his grandmother. It took a lot of convincing, but finally, he started the process which was somewhat repetitive. You see, Billy had a list a mile long of all his grandmother's infractions and he needed to forgive her for each and every one of them. Each time he forgave her, you could sense that he was gaining his freedom. After this emotionally exhausting session, Billy looked like a new man. The anger that once enslaved him, seemed to have disappeared from his countenance, replacing it with peace. Now, he knew what it meant to be free, totally free, and to live life to the fullest for the first time in over ten years.

After a few months had passed, friends got an update from Heather. Billy and Grace had moved about four hours away and by all indications, they were doing great. They had settled into their new apartment, landed new jobs, but the most important thing was that Billy was experiencing a new life of emotional freedom.

Billy was no longer a runner. He was restored.

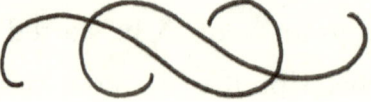

What do you gain when the Lord speaks to you, gives you a command and yet you go in the opposite direction? What if you run away in total disobedience? What does it feel like to be imprisoned for three days, in total darkness, with smelly dead fish all around you? Ask Jonah what it was like. He has a pretty vivid recollection of just that.

'The word of the Lord came to Jonah the son of Amittai saying, *"Arise, go to Nineveh the great city and cry against it, for their wickedness has come up before Me."* But Jonah rose up to flee to Tarshish from the presence of the Lord. So he went down to Joppa, found a ship which was going to Tarshish, paid the fare and went down into it to go with them to Tarshish from the presence of the Lord. The Lord hurled a great wind on the sea and there was a great storm on the sea so that the ship was about to break up. Each man said to his mate, "Come, let us cast lots so we may learn on whose account this calamity has struck us." So they cast lots* *and the lot fell on Jonah. He said to them, "I am a Hebrew, and I fear the Lord God of heaven who made the sea and the dry land." So they said to him, "What should we do to you that the sea may become calm for us?"-for the sea was becoming increasingly stormy. He said to them, "Pick me up and throw me into the sea. Then the sea will become calm for you, for I know that on account of me this great storm has come upon you." So they picked up Jonah, threw him into the sea, and the sea stopped its raging. And the Lord appointed a great fish to swallow Jonah, and Jonah was in the stomach of the fish three days and three nights.'* Jonah 1:1-4,7,9,11-12,15,17

Jonah was commanded by the Lord to go to Nineveh and evangelize, but Jonah had a different idea. He didn't like the idea of spending time with the Ninevites. Put it simply, he rebelled and ran away. When he was confronted with a challenge, he chose to go the opposite direction and run away.

Now, I'm not saying that Billy was like Jonah, or vice versa, but what I am saying is that running from what you should do has its consequences. Billy, not confronting his past and anger issues, faced some negative relationship consequences. When he eventually became obedient and forgave those who hurt him, his life changed. When Jonah confessed his sin of rebellion and disobedience, God restored him as well and there was an enormous revival in Nineveh.

What's the moral to the story? Don't run from God or your problems, you most likely will not like the consequences. Think about the years wasted by Billy, holding onto bitterness and anger. Think about all the joy that he missed out on.

If you do run, or are currently running, STOP! God wants to use you in a huge way and He can't do so if you are running in a different direction. Pay attention to where God is working, as that just may be where He wants you to be as well.

Empty

Jenny was your typical 20ish year old woman with the world in front of her. She was out on her own with a good job and a cute boyfriend. Life couldn't have been any better for her.

While Jenny and her boyfriend had a good relationship, they both knew it wasn't the "forever kind".

One day, Jenny woke up to an upset stomach that got progressively worse. Every day for a couple of weeks it was the same thing. Several times she woke up with the intense urge to throw up. What in the world was going on, she thought? Day after day, she felt horrible. Jenny had no idea what to do. Many mornings, she woke up sick and attributed it to a little too much wine the night before. After a couple of weeks with the same symptoms, she gave up the wine, but nothing changed at all. She talked with some friends, but they were of little help. Jenny thought about talking with her mom, but with her moving out, their relationship was a little strained.

She finally got up the courage to call her mom and talk. While the initial part of the conversation was light hearted, Jenny finally got up the nerve to share her problem.

After her mom had listened for a few minutes without saying a word, she then asked a very straight forward question. "Jenny, are you sleeping with your boyfriend?" "No, we broke up about a month ago." Jenny replied. "Were you?" asked her mom. "Well, yes", Jenny responded reluctantly. There was an awkward pause. Finally, her mom broke the silence. "Well Jenny, I think you need to make a doctor's appointment soon. I believe you are pregnant." Jenny immediately burst out in tears. "I can't be pregnant. I'm not married, and my boyfriend just broke up with me. What am I going to do?"

The next few weeks were tumultuous to say the least. Jenny's thoughts focused on how she would care for a baby. How could she afford it? What would people think? She couldn't take it anymore, so she decided to talk with someone and find out her options. Jenny decided to call a women's clinic and scheduled an appointment for the following day. They seemed so nice on the phone.

The next day, she was in their office with a counselor. First things first, Jenny had a pregnancy test. They confirmed that she was indeed about seven weeks pregnant. That explained everything. The conversation with the counselor was short and to the point. "We can take care of this problem and have you out of here in a few hours." the counselor said. With little thought, discussion or reaction, Jenny was whisked back to another room. Within a few minutes, her "problem" was taken care of. Jenny was no longer pregnant. The counselor simply told her to just go home and rest for a day or so. Initially, she left with a sense of relief and that was about it.

A few days passed before Jenny had a conversation with her mom again. "How are you doing," she asked. Jenny, in a very sullen voice responded, "Oh, I'm ok." Jenny's mom could sense that there was more going on than just the pregnancy and pressed for Jenny to talk more. "Jenny, is something else going on?" Jenny denied anything else. She just didn't feel like talking.

This went on for several weeks. Every time her mom called to talk, Jenny seemed more and more quiet, even to the point of being depressed. Jenny had lost her joy, and day by day, Jenny felt more empty and with little hope. Her emotions were all over the board. One minute she was quiet, the next depressed, then angry and somewhat toxic. People stopped spending time with her and kept their distance. They never knew which tantrums she would throw. As time went by, she felt all alone and empty.

Jenny's conversations with her mother became very short and angry. Although her mother tried being there for her, every day, Jenny pushed her farther and farther away. No matter what her mother tried, Jenny resisted. She had built a wall around her that was so tall that no one could possibly get to her. Jenny was now in total isolation.

Her overwhelming thought was that she had let down everyone, her mom, friends, herself, but mostly her baby and God. How could she do it? Why did she do it? Why did she go through with having an abortion? Every day, Jenny was sinking further into depression and emptiness. What did she have to live for? Who would want her now? Who would want to even be around her, much less be friends?

Her unofficial due date had come. For a couple of months, she had refused to take calls from anyone she knew, especially her mother. While they hadn't talked about it, her Mom knew that the baby's due date would be about this time, so she decided to show up at her apartment. She knocked on Jenny's door and waited patiently for her to answer. The door slowly opened, and Jenny stood in the doorway for a few moments with her mouth gaping wide open. She couldn't believe her eyes. Suddenly, Jenny lost all composure and collapsed in her mother's arms, sobbing.

After crying a few minutes Jenny wiped her face with her sleeve and invited her mom in to her apartment. After finding a place on the sofa, she looked in her mother's eyes and blurted out, "I killed my baby!! I killed my baby! I didn't know what to do. They were so nice on the phone. They said they could help with my problem. I killed my baby!!" Her mother sat there in quiet disbelief as Jenny continued to pour her heart out. The intensity of pain she heard in Jenny's voice grew by the minute. The realization of the abortion finally hit her, and her mom. All that her mom could do was hold her, and to listen.

After a couple of hours, Jenny fell asleep with her head on her mother's lap, with her mom gently stroking her hair. This was reminiscent of times when she was a little girl and was deeply hurt by a friend or classmate. Mom always seemed to know exactly what to do. Sometimes, the best medicine was simply to have mom hold her and let her cry it out.

For days, Jenny stayed in shock. About the only thing her Mom could do was just to console her as best she could. Day after day, she sat with an empty look on her face. As the days went by, Jenny tried to return to her normal self. The days turned into weeks, and weeks turned into months. While Jenny's life did finally revert to some form of reality, she still felt totally empty. There would be trips to the store that would hit a trigger and Jenny would feel her emptiness all over again, just with the simple sight of a mother holding her newborn. Jenny continued to struggle with her emotional ups and downs until one day she just couldn't take it anymore. She needed help.

Jenny was invited and agreed to go to a Restoration weekend. While she was doing well initially, things became a little tense when they started to peel the personal layers away. Jenny was fine with hiding her "junk" in the closet, but now they wanted her to bring things out into the open for all to see. Several times she was tempted to walk out, but each time she tried, her feet became as heavy as lead. She knew she needed to face her battle sooner rather than later. Now was the time.

As the group was sharing, Jenny simply couldn't take it anymore. With no warning, she just blurted out, "I killed my baby!!! I can't keep it hidden any more. I'm tired of carrying this and running away!" There was a hush in the room. People just sat there listening in shock as she made her pronouncement. But with that came a sigh of relief. Jenny had carried this burden for years, not knowing how to deal with it.

Finally, she felt free again. The group just sat there encouraging her, which was more than what she expected since they all just met. There was no condemnation, but only love and concern from the group.

The next afternoon, Jenny was confronted with another reality. What would her life have been like if she had actually given birth? The group took her through an exercise of living what her reality would have been like. Step by step, Jenny envisioned each phase of her baby's life, from changing diapers, the first day of school, all the way through algebra class and her first boyfriend. Jenny's eyes were opened wide. Through this exercise, Jenny realized that she really was a mommy, and that thought immediately brought on a new set of tears. She went from regret and remorse, to overwhelming joy.

Jenny came to the point that her emptiness had been replaced with joy. She could finally breathe without all the negative emotions. Now what would she do with this new-found freedom?

Well, after a few months went by, and with a tremendous amount of conviction from the Lord, Jenny joined a recovery and support ministry which deals with both women and men who have either been through an abortion or are seriously considering it. So far, Jenny has had a profound impact on 50 to 60 women who chose to keep their babies instead choosing to end the lives of precious little ones. Jenny has said that when a mom decides to carry their baby to term, they all have a special victory dance. It's a celebration.

Jenny was fully restored and able to turn her emptiness into joy and a deep peace that passes all understanding.

"Restore to me the joy of Your salvation and sustain me with a willing spirit." Psalm 51:12

"Simon Peter was following Jesus, and so was another disciple. Now that disciple was known to the high priest, and entered with Jesus into the court of the high priest, but Peter was standing at the door outside. So the other disciple, who was known to the high priest, went out and spoke to the doorkeeper, and brought Peter in. Then the slave-girl who kept the door said to Peter, "You are not also one of this man's disciples, are you?" He said, "I am not." Now the slaves and the officers were standing there, having made a charcoal fire, for it was cold and they were warming themselves; and Peter was also with them, standing and warming himself. The high priest then questioned Jesus about His disciples, and about His teaching. Jesus answered him, "I have spoken openly to the world; I always taught in synagogues and in the temple, where all the Jews

come together; and I spoke nothing in secret. Why do you question Me? Question those who have heard what I spoke to them; they know what I said." When He had said this, one of the officers standing nearby struck Jesus, saying, "Is that the way You answer the high priest?"

So Annas sent Him bound to Caiaphas the high priest. Now Simon Peter was standing and warming himself. So they said to him, "You are not also one of His disciples, are you?" He denied it, and said, "I am not." One of the slaves of the high priest, being a relative of the one whose ear Peter cut off, said, "Did I not see you in the garden with Him?" Peter then denied it again, and immediately a rooster crowed." John 18:15-22,24-27

Peter felt a level of grief that few people ever experience. Jesus had become one of Peter's closest friends, and in the heat of the moment, Peter denied ever knowing who Jesus was to the three people who confronted him. Peter grieved so deeply that he had denied Jesus. How could he live with himself?

Peter immediately started to beat himself up. His denials took him to such emptiness that he could hardly bear it.

After Jesus' resurrection, Peter had a personal encounter with Him, and thankfully, Jesus had compassion on Peter and restored him.

Like Peter, Jenny went on to touch many lives. She was restored, and her emptiness was replaced with joy.

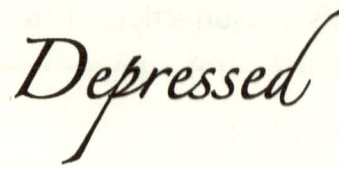

Depressed

Conflict was a way of life with Elizabeth, but not what you would normally think of. Elizabeth was a senior nurse in the critical care unit at the hospital. There were always conflicts between doctors, other nurses, patients and their families, and even the administrators, but these conflicts are generally resolved very quickly. The conflicts usually stemmed from a misdiagnosed problem, procedures to follow, improper communication with the patient's family, and even scheduling issues.

But these aren't the conflicts I'm referring to with Elizabeth. Her conflicts had nothing to do with other people, they were totally internal. They were conflicts she battled subconsciously within herself.

Day after day, Elizabeth found herself second guessing everything she did. Was this the right procedure? Was the patient ready for rehab? Was that the right medication? The patient wants to be released, but are they really ready? Did I tell the family the right thing?

There were times when Elizabeth had to assist in surgical procedures and she found herself second guessing everything she did. Did she follow the doctor's directions properly? She thought. Then there were the conflicts she had with the other nurses. As one of the senior nurses, Elizabeth had some authority over the others, and sometimes, the others resented it when she flexed her authority and would come to terms. That made Elizabeth question every move she made even more. Sometimes she would catch them talking behind her back.

Elizabeth's biggest problem was herself. She was her own worst enemy. She had a problem with being a perfectionist and projected that on everyone around her. It was one thing to correct her subordinate nurses, but to confront doctors with perceived mistakes, was another.

Over time, Elizabeth had managed to alienate just about everyone on her floor. Things got so bad that when it was break time, no one wanted to be around her. If someone was in the nurse's lounge when she walked in, they would often excuse themselves and go to another break room. In no time, word had spread that Elizabeth should be avoided.

Justifiably so, Elizabeth had developed a complex. Sadly, the deeper the complex, the more of a perfectionist she became, alienating people even more. Her friends started avoiding her like a plague.

Her perfectionist attitude started to impact the rest of her life as well, so much so that her boyfriend was starting to back away. They had been together for about two years and Will had always been supportive. He found himself in a somewhat challenging situation. While Will cared for Elizabeth a great deal, he could not deal with her constant badgering over little things. He couldn't seem to do anything right. It wasn't the big things, it was all the little, insignificant issues, and they were starting to take a toll on Will. While they were in a committed relationship, how long would it last? All the criticisms and being corrected was getting to his head. How could he tell Elizabeth how he truly felt? Should he say anything or just walk away and chalk the relationship up to another experience? Of course, Will had his own shortcomings and issues, but how much more of this belittling could he take?

This problem of perfectionism was now impacting literally every aspect of Elizabeth's life, her work, Will, her family and even her friends. When would it end? Was there a breaking point? Someone had to talk to her, but no one had the courage to confront her for fear of getting their heads chopped off.

One day, Elizabeth snapped at the wrong person, or so it seemed. Cheryl and Elizabeth had been friends for over 10 years. They used to do everything together, that was until Will came into the picture. Now Cheryl had taken second fiddle to him, but she didn't mind.

Elizabeth and Cheryl were having a girl's night out. First, they had pizza, then followed by a typical girl's movie. Finally, they went to one of those all-night coffee shops that had jazz music playing in the background. Everyone was dressed as if they had just gotten to town from Woodstock. Great thing though, everyone had a smile on their faces and seemed to be in a good mood.

While enjoying their favorite latte, Elizabeth started to unload on Cheryl, and not long into their chat, Cheryl said the "wrong" thing and Elizabeth lost her cool. "Whoa, what's with you?" Cheryl asked. "Don't even think about talking to me like that." There was a strange pause. "I'm sorry." Elizabeth finally responded. "I just feel so much on edge all the time. It seems like everyone has taken "stupid pills" these days and I don't know how to handle it. Everyone seems to be saying the dumbest things and I'm always having to correct them. What is wrong with people? Is there something in the water that people are drinking?"

Cheryl sat there for a moment and allowed Elizabeth's words to sink in, she wanted to figure out just what to say before she responded. "Elizabeth, you say everyone has been taking stupid pills? Could there be another option?" "What exactly are you saying?" replied Elizabeth. "Well, maybe it isn't everyone else, maybe it's you?" Cheryl quipped. "So, what's going on?"

Elizabeth just sat there with a blank look on her face. After a couple minutes of unexpected silence, she finally answered, "I have no clue! No one seems to like me, Will, people at work, no one! They all seem to be avoiding me." "So how are you doing otherwise? What else is going on?" Cheryl prodded.

As the conversation continued, Elizabeth slipped into a minor breakdown, she had no clue exactly what was happening. Just a few months ago, everything seemed to be going fine. Her relationship with Will was progressing. Her job was doing well, and she had earned a nice promotion to senior nurse on her floor. Her boss was picking on her a little, pointing out everything she was doing wrong, or so it seemed. But other than that, life had been going well. After a little while, an idea came to Cheryl. "About a year ago, I went through this program. Remember that weekend I went down to Texas? Remember how my attitude changed when I came back?" Elizabeth thought for a moment and responded with a strong, "Yes, you were totally different."

Cheryl quickly challenged Elizabeth, "I think you need to attend the same program. In fact, if you and Will are going anywhere with your relationship, I think he should go also." "I don't need that thing." Elizabeth replied, "Maybe you needed it, but not me." Cheryl chuckled a little and responded. "How are you doing at fixing things yourself? You know, I've noticed some things that seem to take you to the edge, but I just didn't want to say anything about it. I think you should strongly consider going to the program. You remember how much more peaceful I was when I got back. I had lost my joy and I was able to get it back while I was there. It opened my eyes to some issues that I didn't even know I had buried. I'll tell you what, I'll text you the numbers tomorrow. I think you should strongly consider going to the program, I really think you would get a lot out of the weekend."

Elizabeth just sat there for a moment, not saying a thing. "Well, let me talk with Will, he probably needs it more than I do. I'll let you know whatever we decide. "Cheryl sat there with a smile on her face, she knew what Elizabeth was about to go through.

The next evening, Elizabeth and Will were finishing their dinner when she said, "Guess what we are doing in two weeks? We are going to Texas for the weekend. Cheryl said we needed to go to this seminar thing, and that it will be good for us." Will sat there with a blank look on his face. "What are you talking about? What seminar? What prompted this craziness?" "I'll get Cheryl on the phone so she can explain everything." Elizabeth assured.

And with that, Elizabeth and Will made plans to head south for a weekend. Living in northern Oklahoma, it would be about a four and a half hour drive just to get there.

The next couple of weeks went by fast and before you knew it, the travel day had finally come. Although there was some resistance from both of them, Cheryl was steadfast in her insistence that they should attend, so off they went.

They arrived late in the afternoon and checked in to their hotel and the seminar. All they knew was that Cheryl told them they would love it and would be better after it was finished. Thankfully, Cheryl and Elizabeth had a lot of miles behind them as friends.

As the seminar started, both of them sat in the room with a group of total strangers, getting more anxious by the minute. "What are we doing here?" Elizabeth whispered to Will. Shortly after she said that, one of the leaders up front reminded everyone, "There will be no side conversations during the weekend." Wow, Elizabeth took that personally. "He doesn't even know me and already he's attacking me, how rude of him." she thought.

Saturday morning started off fast. The large group had been broken down to smaller groups of four or five people the night before. Elizabeth found herself in a group of five women of all ages. Cindy was the youngest at 23, Elizabeth the second oldest at 54 and Mary was 59.

Elizabeth's wall went up a little higher that morning. What could she possibly get from all these younger women? The leaders started probing for things. "Tell us about when you felt like a victim. Tell us about being rejected. And so on." Elizabeth decided that she really didn't want to play this game and shut down even more. Unfortunately, it was her time to share. Arms crossed, she told a story that had nothing to do with anything. Everyone looked at her bewildered. Her group leader looked at her and said, "I thought you came for some help in fixing some life issues."

That became a pattern for Elizabeth, keep the walls up so no one could see her weaknesses. That didn't sit too well with Hank, one of the leaders of the program who often went from one group to the next, just listening and observing each person. Hank built an arsenal of sorts to use at a later time to help restore people.

After a lot of encouragement, Elizabeth finally revealed that her father had set a standard so high for her while she was growing up, not even Superwoman could live up to it. Finally, she made progress, and there was something to work with in helping her have a breakthrough. It was about that time that Hank was there observing. He reached into his arsenal and confronted Elizabeth with her reality.

"Elizabeth, I have a question for you. How long have you been a perfectionist?" Hank probed. Stunned, Elizabeth replied, "Since I was a little girl. My father was in the Marines and he drilled it into my head that nothing less than perfect was acceptable." With a little levity Hank responded, "How's that working for you?" Elizabeth sat there in shock for a moment. No one had ever confronted her like that before. She didn't know what to say or think. Hank continued by asking, "Elizabeth, will you ever be perfect?" "Well, no, I guess not." She replied. "Do you know anyone who is perfect?" Hank continued to question. Again, Elizabeth responded with a, "No." "May I ask you another question?" Hank said. "I guess so, you are going to anyway." Elizabeth said with a smile on her face. The whole group chuckled a little. Everyone knew basically where Hank was going with this line of questions. "Why are you trying to be perfect? Why not change that to striving for excellence?" Hank posed. "If you strive for excellence, you will amaze yourself and sometimes you will hit perfection. Here's the best part about this thought process, you will relieve yourself of the pressure and actually have a lot more enjoyment along the way. Who knows, people may even start to like you again since you aren't putting excessive pressure on them."

Elizabeth simply stood there with a surprised look on her face. "I've never considered that before. Why has no one ever suggested this to me?" She asked. "Maybe you were so focused on being perfect, you couldn't hear any other alternatives. Maybe you just weren't ready to get out of your own way?" Hank said, then just walked away. His work was just about complete with Elizabeth. He got her thinking about a new paradigm that would restore her peace and her confidence.

The weekend progressed with others having huge breakthroughs. Some in the areas of forgiving people who had wronged them, others getting to the point of recognizing who they were in God's eyes.

For Hank, the weekend concluded on a high note, and a confirmation that he was right where he needed to be. Will and Elizabeth came to him when the seminar ended to thank him. Will reached out for a typical hug. Elizabeth however, hugged but wouldn't let go. With tears in her eyes, she said, "You changed my life, you restored my joy and confidence. I will remember what you said about excellence versus perfection forever. I can't thank you enough for pulling me out of the dark pit of depression I had fallen into. I have some major apologies to make when I get back home."

Hank responded, "Elizabeth, you did the heavy lifting, I just gave you a tool to help out. Thank you for being willing to listen to something new. Go and be a blessing to others and show them grace when they aren't perfect. Have grace with yourself when you aren't perfect. Just strive for excellence and you will have joy."

For Elizabeth, she had to forgive herself for all her shortcomings, but more importantly, she had to remind herself that only Jesus is perfect. Her new word of the day, every day, is excellence.

"Who among you is wise and understanding? Let him show by his good behavior his deeds in the gentleness of wisdom. But if you have bitter jealousy and selfish ambition in your heart, do not be arrogant and so lie against the truth. This wisdom is not that which comes down from above, but is earthly, natural, demonic. For where jealousy and selfish ambition exist, there is disorder and every evil thing. But the wisdom from above is first pure, then peaceable, gentle, reasonable, full of mercy and good fruits, unwavering, without hypocrisy. And the seed whose fruit is righteousness is sown in peace by those who make peace." James 3:13-18

Elizabeth's problem was centered around her aspirations of being perfect. In the above verses, James talks about bitter jealousy, selfish ambition, arrogance and lying against the truth. They bring disorder and every evil thing. Wisdom from above is first pure, peaceable, good fruits and without hypocrisy.

This example is in contrast with perfectionism, which is generally based in self-centeredness. Excellence has a foundation in wisdom. Which are you striving for today? Elizabeth chose excellence. What are you striving for today?

More stories of Restoration and grace.

Hank's Story

Hank had been dealing with self-worth issues for many years. It stemmed from being the youngest of four boys in his family. His older brothers were constantly putting him down and picking on him. He managed to overcome the belittling most of the time, but he occasionally struggled with who he was when he looked at himself in the mirror. Who did he actually see?

When Hank was 16 years old, he was confronted with the reality of who Jesus is, and decided to follow Jesus and made Him Lord of his life.

A few years later, Hank got married to a woman he met in college. While the marriage was going well, or so he thought, Hank's wife didn't know the power of her words and the Biblical principal of honoring your husband.

One day, Hank had an appointment with a prospective client. While he was there to propose one service to this company, Allen, the president changed courses in mid-stream.

For many years, Hank had been working with other clients to help grow their businesses by utilizing the products he offered. He had been dreaming about helping companies with his creative marketing ideas. His door had now been opened with Allen who asked Hank if he would help him devise a strategic marketing plan for his technical school. To say Hank was excited would be a huge understatement.

That evening, Hank overflowed with excitement about his new opportunity, and he simply couldn't contain himself. The moment his wife walked through the door, he started to share immediately. It was almost like he was bouncing off the wall. In spite of his excitement, Hank's wife managed to take all the wind out of his sails with two simple, but very painful and condescending questions, "Why would anyone want *you* to do anything like that for them? What do *you* know about that?"

It became obvious that in the 12 years they had been married, she didn't pay a lot of attention to what he did in his job. In the previous ten years, he worked with business owners, helping them to refine their messages and help them grow their organizations. Now, his wife deflated him so much, it was as if he was cut off at the knees. Immediately, Hank went into a tailspin that affected him for years. His self-confidence took a major hit. How could he believe in himself when the person he trusted the most took away his wind?

For the next 18 years, Hank had an artificial ceiling put over him by the words his wife spoke. Sadly enough, he believed what his wife said and subconsciously started to put limits on himself. He stopped striving for excellence and started settling for average.

Years after this incident, different friends started encouraging Hank to go through the Restoration program. Initially, he said he was working on his own self improvement program and didn't really need it. Finally, the timing was right for him to attend.

At the beginning of each year, Hank always went through some type of personal development program to start the year off right. Hank's primary objective in going through the program was to figure out why he had hit a plateau and then get beyond it. This would be the best time to embark on the Restoration experience. It was mid-November and the next session wasn't scheduled until the second week of January. The next eight weeks couldn't come fast enough for him.

The January weekend had finally arrived, and Hank was ready. He didn't really know what he was in for, no one would share any details. All people had told him was that it was different for everyone.

On Friday evening, Hank was there with a group of about 60 other people, waiting to see what they had gotten themselves into. Hank had prepared himself for the weekend, knowing he had to let his guard down as much as possible. By doing that, he knew that it would be the only way he would achieve a breakthrough.

As the large group broke into smaller groups, Hank started implementing some self-talk, trying to encourage himself to be strong. On the outside, Hank was generally pretty confident and strong, but on the inside, Hank was shaking like a leaf. How vulnerable does he need to be?

Right out of the chute, they started probing. "Tell us about a time you felt like a victim." Wow, he didn't see that coming. He had a pretty shallow response. The next question came. "Tell us about a time you felt rejected." Hank was in a group of five others and he was right in the middle as the third person in his circle. Thankfully, that meant he had a little bit of time to think of something. All of a sudden, Hank had a vivid flashback. It took him straight back to that incident when his now ex-wife criticized him about the marketing project.

They say that our memories are tied to emotional events, and this was definitely one. The memory came back in full color. He remembered every single detail, especially how he felt then, and he didn't like how he now felt. Hank thought that feeling was long gone. "Why are these goofy people making me dredge this up?" He thought. His emotions were all over the place. First was the hurt and depression, then the anger. Hank had been suppressing this feeling for a long time.

"Alright, you got me to remember something ugly from my past. Now what?" Hank said as he didn't know what to do with this ugliness. They told him to think about how he felt and what the anger was doing to him inside.

This exercise was near the end of the evening session. The leaders of the large group made everyone hold on to their ugliness overnight and they would deal with it the next day. They didn't actually say that, but Hank had been through enough programs, he knew what was happening.

The next morning couldn't arrive fast enough. Hank wanted to jettison his feelings as fast as possible, but before he could do that, they had more exercises to go through. Finally, the time had come. Let's get rid of this junk, he thought. The leaders started talking about the best way the participants could deal with their victimization and rejection.

Hank was starting to get a little agitated and anxious at the same time. "Okay, let's get on with it."

After about 20minutes of discussion, they decided that forgiveness was the best path to take in order to get resolution. "Well, duh." Hank said to himself. He already thought of that. But there was a specific process they were all supposed to go through, and Hank couldn't wait to learn what that was. He wanted to get rid of the ugly memory as fast as possible.

Around the circle they go. But this time was a little different. Each participant was asked to volunteer when they were ready. Hank was ready and raring to go. "Let's get this over and done." Within a few minutes, Hank had identified his source of pain and went through the process of forgiveness. He had to forgive his ex-wife for not believing in him. He had to forgive her for the ugly, condescending words she spoke that day, words of rejection he had carried for the past 18 years.

Finally, Hank was free, as if his chains of bondage were broken. The barrier had been shattered. The ceiling was lifted off of him. No more looking over his shoulders and replaying those hurtful words. Up is now the only direction to go. This is what it feels like to be free.

Elijah was a mighty prophet of God. He walked with God and had great faith in the God of Abraham, Isaac and Jacob. One day, the prophets of Baal were mocking Elijah and his God. Baal's prophets numbered about 450 men. Elijah decided to show them who God really is and challenged them to a burning of the oxen. Baal's prophets prepared an ox to be sacrificed, and they chanted and called out to their gods. Nothing happened. They called for fire to consume their sacrifice, but no fire came from their gods throughout the day.

Now it was Elijah's turn. He rebuilt the altar, prepared the ox and placed it on the altar. Next, he had the prophets douse it with water, so much so that it was saturated, as was the ground around it.

Elijah then called out to God to show Himself and to send down fire to totally consume everything. God did as Elijah asked. Everything was consumed by the One true God. Gone were the oxen, altar, even the water that was on the ground under the sacrifice.

Elijah then went to battle with all of the prophets of Baal and slew them all.1 Kings 18:20-40

Ahab was not happy and went to Jezebel to tell her what had happened. She sent a messenger to Elijah to tell him his days were numbered. In fear, Elijah took off running as fast as he could to get away from her. He ran to Beersheba with his servants and left them there.

Elijah went another day's journey into the wilderness and came and sat under a juniper tree. Fear had taken over the mighty prophet. Exhausted, Elijah fell asleep under the tree, and there an angel tended to his needs and he was refreshed and strengthened.

Elijah felt all alone, but God sent him on his way, renewed and restored his strength and gave him a new mission.

Elijah had listened to the words of Jezebel and became fearful, but God restored him.

Hank, was like Elijah, he was restored when God confronted him with the truth once again. Hank found himself listening to the lies of the world. When he stopped listening to the negative words, he was able to see who he was in God's eyes. He was no longer trapped by the negative words that replayed in his head over and over. Hank quickly realized that he was a "Worthy child of God." This became his mantra which played over and over in his head throughout the day, every day. Hank had replaced the negative worldly words, with the truth of who he really was.

Redeemed

Over the years, Hank had the incredible pleasure of working with a lot of people. Some were severely wounded because of physical, mental, or even sexual abuse. There were those who had major self-image issues, while others felt abandoned. Then there was Ben. He was a real piece of work. To say that he was filled with self-confidence would be like comparing the Gulf of Mexico to a cup of water. No matter what we were talking about, Ben knew the subject matter, or so he thought.

Ben grew up in the city, with all the hustle and bustle. His high school had over 2,500 students. Ben was one of the co-captains on his high school football team, even though he was the runt of the team. He compensated for his small stature by making sure everyone knew he was in charge of everything. There were times he suffered from "Small Man Syndrome"; sometimes cocky or arrogant, all the time overly confident.

Ben graduated from high school and went on to a top-rated university majoring in Management. He was determined to be in charge no matter where he was.

With a 3.9 GPA, Ben graduated and got a job in the accounting department of a fortune 1,000 company. While he started at the bottom, within the first year, he had received three promotions and was now a departmental manager. Ben had found his spot in life. He felt as though he was in charge and going in the right direction. Ben knew he was in charge of his destiny.

While Ben would have minor setbacks from time to time, he always knew how to make his way back to the top, and very quickly at that.

For several years, Ben had been competing in Mudders. These are team obstacle courses where you encounter some very intense terrain and yes, a lot of mud. You always knew who the participants were, they were covered from head to toe in mud. At the Mudder events you had three types of people; participants, organizers, and bystanders. There were those who helped put the event on, and those who just liked coming to encourage the crazy people in the event.

Along came Becky. She was one of the bystanders, or in her case, cheerleader. She didn't care who it was, she was shouting out encouraging words.

Instantly, Ben was distracted by Becky. She was 25 years old, a cute brunette with a contagious personality. For the next several months, Ben and Becky had become an inseparable pair. They had become a "thing" almost overnight.

By then, Ben was 28 years old and he had decided that he was ready to settle down and get married. Their courtship and engagement period lasted a grand total of five months. Ben's new life had begun.

What was once Ben's idea of being in charge of everything in his life, quickly became a battle. Becky had also been an "in charge" person and had determined that she would be in charge of the house. Initially, they tried to work things out in a gracious manner, but that lasted about a year. Neither of the two liked giving in, they thought it would show a sign of weakness.

On the surface, especially when they were out in public, they appeared to be a good, fun-loving couple with not a single problem. The constant competition in the home, along with the never-ending bickering was really starting to take its toll on both of them. They became more and more distant. Ben even built a man cave, so he wouldn't have to spend as much time with Becky.

One day, Becky suggested that they go for counseling to try to work things out. At first, Ben pushed back and refused to go. She finally wore him down and Ben conceded. This didn't last long though, he felt that the sessions were nothing but a time to beat up on him, two against one now. Ben wanted nothing to do with this game she was playing.

After five years of this misery, Ben decided to call it quits. "Where is this marriage going?" he would ask himself. No place! Ben was out.

Initially it was just a separation, but after about six months, Ben filed for divorce. Three months later, Ben and Becky were no more, and he was finally free to do what he wanted again. He could be in control, or so he thought. This was the beginning of Ben's spiral down to a place he had never known before.

Ben started to jump from relationship to relationship. He was looking for a perfect relationship but couldn't quite figure out exactly what that relationship looked like. In reality, he had lost who he was and was trying to find himself all over again. Sadly, this was at the expense of a number of other women who were left behind if they didn't measure up.

After several years of his aimless lifestyle, Ben found himself feeling totally lost and out of control, failing in just about everything. He went through four jobs in six years and couldn't seem to accomplish anything. The once self-confident Ben had become a "yes man", trying to figure out where to go next.

Along the way, Ben and Tracy became friends. Once they were co-workers, but now just good friends. There was never anything romantic with the two of them, they just enjoyed their friendship and were and confidants to each other. One day, the two got together for their monthly catch-up dinner. Tracy immediately noticed that there was something going on with Ben, so she started to probe. Reluctantly, Ben shared his story including his lack of confidence and feeling lost. It was as if he was just wandering through life at this point. Then there was the issue of him not being able to hold on to any sort of relationship.

That was all Tracy needed to know. She was one who wouldn't hold back with Ben. Most people were afraid to share the truth with him for fear that he would bite their heads off in a moment's notice. Not Tracy though, she called it as she saw it.

"Ben, you are messed up in a big way and you need help." Tracy said. Ben quickly snapped back, "What are you talking about? I'm just in a little valley right now, I'll get out of it." Tracy quickly replied, "Ben, you've been like this for months and you aren't getting any better." With that, Ben started putting his defenses up and bristled, "I've got things under control and. I don't need anyone's help." Tracy, with a little smirk on her face retorted, "Really, how's that working for you? Ben, you are so stubborn and arrogant at times. You think you know everything. Right now, the way I see it, you don't know anything. You do remember that I help all kinds of people with all kinds of issues, don't you?" Tracy continued. "Ben, you need to go through Restoration. I don't say this to many people, but you are messed up and you need this program, and you need it fast. I'm calling tomorrow to get you registered for the next session. I believe it is in two weeks. Don't argue with me!"

With that, their discussion about the program was over, Tracy had won this round. The next day, she called and registered Ben and it was a done deal.

The next couple of weeks couldn't get there fast enough. Ben was actually starting to look forward to the program, he was tired of living in a pit and not being able to get out of it.

The day of the program had arrived. As a counselor, Tracy was sitting this weekend out to give Ben plenty of space to deal with his issues. Normally, Tracy would be right in the thick of things helping other people overcome their challenges. She loved the work and found a lot of fulfillment in it. She had dealt with an ugly divorce years earlier herself and found tremendous healing by going through Restoration. Now she gets to help others through their own junk.

It's Friday evening and all the program participants were there sitting in this big meeting room. People from all backgrounds and walks of life were there, all trying to figure out who these strangers were and why everyone was together.

After about an hour, all the opening gibberish was shared. "What did it all mean? Who were these people standing around the perimeter of the room? I thought this was a seminar. I thought I would be taking notes, or something." Ben thought to himself.

"Finally, it's break time. I don't need this junk. I'm out of here," He thought. As he left the room, Ben was quickly confronted by Tracy. "How are you doing? You look like you want to leave." Tracy challenged. Tracy knew Ben would try to run if he wasn't in control. She conveniently put herself in the hallway outside the doors in case he did try to escape. "You know the answers to your problems are inside the room. If you leave now, how will you find them? It's your choice." Tracy said. "I haven't seen you as a quitter before. Will this be your time?

Ben was really annoyed. To him, it seemed like he was in a fortress. He couldn't run. What would it do to their friendship? With her challenge, he really had no choice but to return and keep his word about completing the program.

When the group returned to the room, they were split into smaller groups. The people that were standing around were the facilitators who oversaw the smaller groups. Their roles were to keep the people talking and ask them lots of questions. One of their favorite questions was, "So, how's that working for you?" Another question that they asked a lot was, "How does that make you feel?"

Ben's facilitator was Hank. When this small group thing started, Hank seemed to be pretty nice and listened intently. After a couple of hours though, Hank seemed to change. He was able to see right through Ben's responses. It was almost as if Hank had some kind of X ray vision that could see what people were hiding. At one point, a question was asked in the group, everyone would be on the hot seat, including Ben. Hank knew that Ben had a wall up and wasn't really emotionally or mentally there. "Ben, how long are you going to hide behind your self-constructed wall?" Hank knew exactly what to say to chisel away at Ben. Somehow, Ben would have to peel away the layers to get to the core of his problems.

One by one, the layers were pulled away and Ben was finally starting to be honest with himself. Hank had uncovered the root cause of one of his issues, his size, and thus his over compensation. Ben was beginning to also realize that he had been wearing a mask for fear that people wouldn't like him if they really got to know him. Come to find out, Ben was really insecure and just played the overly confident person who everyone else saw. He was finally set free that night. He could go home and try to get some sleep.

Saturday morning arrived, and Ben was in for more intense questions. He decided overnight that he really would give it his all. He came in to the meeting room, ready to go. Last night, he jumped a major hurdle just by admitting his insecurities. Now came the tough part.

While Restoration was a Christian-based program, they never forced their particular beliefs on anyone. They did however, want people to have an opportunity to know who God was and is. By this time, Ben had developed a great level of trust with all of those in his small group, including Hank. In fact, he felt safe with them. He hadn't felt safe with many people in a very long time.

As the day progressed, his group was asked who they are in God's eyes? Frankly, Ben had never taken the time to really think about this. Why does he need to know what God thought of him? What difference does it make anyway? He didn't know much about God, just that he had this book of rules and he knew he would never measure up.

The next exercise took Ben in a whole new direction. This was something he never saw coming. "Ben," Hank said, "May I ask you a question?" Ben quickly nodded, not knowing where the conversation was going. "If you were to die today, and you are standing at the Great Pearly Gates to meet Jesus, why should He let you in?" Hank asked. After thinking about it for a minute or so, Ben responded with, "Well, I think I've done more good than bad in my life." Hank thought for a moment and said, "What if I told you it had nothing to do with how good or bad you were? Rather, it had everything to do with the sacrifice Jesus made on the cross and Him forgiving all your sins?" "What do you mean by *all* my sins?" Ben replied. "That's a great question." Hank said. "I mean everything you have done that is against God, all your wrong thoughts and deeds."

Ben stood there for a moment, speechless, then he started shaking his head. "Well, that will never happen. I guess I really have done a lot of bad things in my life, and God could never forgive everything. I've been pretty mean to a lot of people and there are people I've taken advantage of when I shouldn't." Ben admitted.

Hank replied with, "Ben, what sins do you think God didn't or shouldn't forgive? With Hank's question, he stood there with a blank look on his face. No one had ever asked these kinds of questions before. Ben paused for a moment and realized that his friend, Tracy had been asking him these types of questions all the time. He blew them off by saying to himself, "I don't need your religion, that's good for you, not me."

Hank asked, "Ben, what if I told you that you could release yourself from your past right now and ask God to forgive all your sins?" With a puzzled look on his face, Ben said, "How do I do that?" Hank looked to the front of the room where there was a large cross hanging on the wall and said, "Come with me."

While they started heading toward the cross, Hank picked up a box of tissues. Along with Ben, the others from his small group followed Hank to the front of the room. With Ben facing the cross, Hank finished sharing the Good News about God's forgiveness and how it sets us free.

Now came the time of reckoning. Hank asked Ben a simple but point-blank question. "What sins have you committed that you think God could not forgive? I want you to name each one while you pull out a tissue. Then I want you to simply drop it to the floor as if that is God forgiving the sin you committed. "Right off the bat, Ben was naming some pretty superficial sins, like arguing with his parents, cussing, speeding, shoplifting and so on.

Hank responded with an affirmation that he was going in the right direction. "Good so far Ben, now let's get to the meat of things. You said there were things you had done that you thought God could never forgive. Let's get them out, as it will help you to release all the guilt and shame you are carrying on the inside."

All of a sudden, Ben grabbed a tissue and started sharing some pretty ugly things. "God, please forgive me for..." The confessions went on for about 10 minutes. With each sin, Ben cried harder. Most of the issues revolved around his ex-wife, Becky. For the first time, he realized how cruel he was to her. His tears were almost uncontrollable as he looked down to see the pile of tissues which represented his forgiven sins. Now Ben was beginning to breathe a little more freely.

After Ben had been there for a few minutes, Hank asked a simple question. "If you were to be standing before God at the end of your life and He asked why He should let you into His heaven, what would you say?" Ben meekly and simply said, "Because Jesus took ALL my sins with Him on the cross. He forgave me!"

Ben started to sob once again. "I can't believe how cruel I was to Becky. She was just trying to be a good wife. She tried to tell me about Jesus, but I wouldn't listen, I was so arrogant and full of myself. I can't believe how much I hurt her. I hope she will be able to forgive me, I know I don't deserve it though. She has every right to hate me after all the things I said and did to her."

Hank looked at Ben and said, "Ben, I think you got what you were looking for at Restoration. What do you think you need to do with this new found relationship with Jesus and understanding of forgiveness? Ben looked over at Hank and said, "How do I fix things with Becky? How do I get her back? I was so wrong." Hank responded by encouraging Ben, "One step at a time. Let's get you a little more healed. You will know when the time is right to share with Becky. If she is a Christ follower as you think she is, I believe she will welcome your admission. Who knows, maybe she has already forgiven you. You won't know until you visit with her and share your Good News."

"First thing though," Hank started saying, "I want you to pick up all your junk from the floor." Ben quickly bent down and picked up all the discarded tissues. He stood there holding them for a moment and with a look of curiosity, Hank asked, "Why are you holding on to your sin tissues?" Without hesitation, Ben responded, "You told me to pick them up." "Ben, isn't that what life is like? Someone tells you to go back to a pattern of sin and you willingly do it," Hank replied. "You have to learn to cast away your sin and leave it in your past. Don't keep picking it up. It is in your past now. You need to just leave it there and learn to walk away. Otherwise, you will fall into the pattern of going back to your old lifestyle. It is kind of like a dog returning to its own vomit. Is that what you want to do? Or do you want to start a new life and move forward?"

Ben got the point and quickly dropped the tissues and began to stomp on them, almost as if to say that he was done with them and leaving them behind.

A few weeks later, Ben had a chance to deeply consider all he had been through in the Restoration program, and he prayed about what he should do about Becky. He was determined to do the right thing by her.

It had been seven years since Ben had been in contact with Becky, and he wasn't quite sure where she was. Was she in any kind of a relationship? Had she remarried? None of that really mattered. Ben had to share with Becky what he had experienced and seek her forgiveness.

Ben picked up his phone, took a big breath and dialed her number but then immediately hung up the phone, he couldn't do it. Maybe he should send her an email or a text? Once again, he picked up the phone and dialed her number. After three rings, Becky answered the phone. The lump in Ben's throat was about the size of a softball.

"Ummm, Becky? Ah, this is Ben. How've you been?" He said in a clumsy manner. There was silence on the other end of the phone for a few seconds. Finally, Becky responded, "I'm fine. What can I do for you?" "Well, I was wondering if we could get together for coffee or something. I have something I need to share with you." Ben said in a very sheepish manor. "Ben, why do we need to get together? Can't you just say what you have to say over the phone?" she replied. "I can, but I really think I should tell you this in person. Please, I promise, this won't take long, but I really need to see you. Can we meet tomorrow evening at the old coffee shop where we used to go?" He asked. Becky thought for a moment and responded, "I'll give you 30 minutes and not a minute longer. I think we have said everything we need to say to each other." "What time?" she asked. "How does 7:30 work? I know you like to go to the gym. I don't want to keep you from that." Ben answered. "I'll see you then. Bye." And with that Becky hung up and went back to what she was doing.

The next evening, Ben arrived at the coffee shop early, petrified. He had rehearsed what he was going to say so many times. He said it in his head one last time before Becky got there.

As she walked through the door, Ben quickly got up and helped her with her chair. The small talk started as Becky looked at her watch. "I said I would give you 30 minutes and I mean it. Let's get on with it." she said.

"First, I have to tell you about a weekend I had a few weeks ago. I went to this program called Restoration. And, well, I asked Jesus to forgive me and I asked Him to come into my life. I'm not quite sure what that means, I just know that I feel totally different." Becky quickly replied, "Ben, I'm happy for you. Is that what you needed to say? Why couldn't you tell me this over the phone?"

With his head bowed a little, Ben said, "Well that is just part of it. I wanted to tell you in person how sorry I am for treating you the way I did for all those years. You didn't deserve my abuse. I'm so ashamed of everything I did. I treated you like dirt, and I'm sorry. I hope you will find it within yourself to someday forgive me. I know I was wrong. If you don't want to, I completely understand. I don't want anything from you and don't expect anything either. I just needed to confess to you and tell you how sorry I am."

Becky just sat there, stunned and speechless for a few minutes. "Ben, you need to know that I forgave you a long time ago. I knew you were messed up and needed Christ in your life. You just wouldn't listen to me when I tried to share Him with you."

Ben said, "I realize now what you were doing, I just didn't want to hear it then. I was too hung up on myself that I wouldn't listen. I'm so sorry for hurting you so much. My biggest problem now is forgiving myself for the way I treated you. They told me it would take some time to do that, but I'm trying hard."

"Ben, if God forgave you and I forgave you, who are you to not forgive yourself? Doesn't that make you bigger than God if you don't?" She said. Ben, with a stunned look on his face said, "Wow, I never thought of things that way. There I go again with my arrogance and self-centeredness. I have a lot to learn. Umm, well, that's what I wanted to tell you. Thank you for listening. I know you have things to do so I'll let you go. I'm just going to sit here for a little while, I've got a lot of things to think about. I'm making a list of other people I need to apologize to as well. You were at the top of the list though."

"I don't really have to leave if you want to talk more." Becky responded. "By the way, you should know, the whole time we were together, I was forgiving you along the way. I probably shouldn't say this but I'm going to anyway. I never stopped praying for you and I never stopped loving you. I just hoped that you got what you were looking for with your life."

"Wow! I'm speechless." Ben muttered. "Um, could I see you again, maybe, ah sometime next week?" "We'll see, I need to do some processing myself. There is a possibility. No commitments right now. I'll let you know later in the week." Becky replied.

Ben and Becky started dating weeks later and were determined to take things slowly this time. While Becky had already forgiven Ben, there were still some wounds that needed to be healed. Becky and Ben had lost hope in their relationship. Little by little, that hope was being restored because Ben had been redeemed.

Ben was living a life of legalism instead of grace. He thought God was judging him based on the things he did or didn't do. The Apostle Paul challenged the Christians in Galatia with this very thing. Were they living under the law, or were they living under Grace?

"You foolish Galatians, who has bewitched you, before whose eyes Jesus Christ was publicly portrayed as crucified? This is the only thing I want to find out from you: did you receive the Spirit by the works of the Law, or by hearing with faith? Are you so foolish? Having begun by the Spirit, are you now being perfected by the flesh? Did you suffer so many things in vain-if indeed it was in vain? So then, does He who provides you with the Spirit and works miracles among you, do it by the works of the Law, or by hearing with faith? Even so Abraham BELIEVED GOD, AND IT WAS RECKONED TO HIM AS RIGHTEOUSNESS. Therefore, be sure that it is those who are of faith who are sons of Abraham. The Scripture, foreseeing that God would justify the Gentiles by faith, preached the gospel beforehand to Abraham, saying, " ALL THE NATIONS WILL BE BLESSED IN YOU. " So then those who are of faith are blessed with Abraham, the believer. For as many as are of the works of the Law are under a curse; for it is written, "CURSED IS EVERYONE WHO DOES NOT ABIDE BY ALL THINGS WRITTEN IN THE BOOK OF THE

LAW, TO PERFORM THEM." Now that no one is justified by the Law before God is evident; for, " THE RIGHTEOUS MAN SHALL LIVE BY FAITH." However, the Law is not of faith; on the contrary, " HE WHO PRACTICES THEM SHALL LIVE BY THEM." Christ redeemed us from the curse of the Law, having become a curse for us-for it is written, " CURSED IS EVERYONE WHO HANGS ON A TREE "- in order that in Christ Jesus the blessing of Abraham might come to the Gentiles, so that we would receive the promise of the Spirit through faith." Galatians 3:1-14

When you live under the Law, you will constantly be looking over your shoulder, waiting for God to zap you. What if He zaps you at the wrong time? What if you are "good" 23.5 hours in a day, and that one-half hour you go down the wrong path? Do you get zapped for that one 30-minute period? What about all the time you were good? That's what you get with the Law.

What if you are living under God's grace? When Jesus died on the cross of Calvary, He took ALL of our sins. When I say ALL, that means ALL. That even includes those sins we have not yet committed. After all, two thousand years ago, our sins were ALL in the future.

Because God cannot even look at sin, He had to offer the perfect sacrifice in Jesus. He bore our sins so that we would be perfect in God's eyes. He actually sees us through Jesus.

If your entrance into eternity with God is dependent upon you being perfect, the only way to do it is with a perfect substitute.

Under the Law, you can strive to be perfect, however, Paul says in Romans, "*For all have sinned and fall short of the glory of God,*" Romans 3:23

So, where are you? Are you living under the Law, or are you walking in God's grace? There is true peace in knowing that Thee God of heaven and earth loves you just as you are. He may not like the things you say and do at times, but if you have accepted His sacrifice, you are in His Kingdom forever and nothing can separate you from His eternal love. No matter how good or bad you are, He will never love you more and never love you less. That is God's grace!

The Answer

Have you ever dropped a precious pitcher, bowl, or cup and it broke into many pieces? What if it was your favorite item? What if you were the item that was dropped or kicked to the side? Once you were useful, but now, because you have been "damaged", you feel as though you have little or no value to others any longer.

Unlike Humpty Dumpty, when you fall and break into many pieces, you can be put back together again. You won't be the same as before, you'll have rough edges and deformed spots, but you can be used again.

How is this possible you ask? God has some *Super Glue* that we don't have, unless you get it through Him. He calls that glue Forgiveness, Restoration, and Freedom.

The great thing about *God's Super Glue*, it generally makes us stronger. When God puts our pieces back together, hopefully we have learned our lessons and repented of our wrong doings. There are a lot of lessons we learn as well when others do something that hurts us. Hopefully we learn from those lessons also.

Many years ago, I found myself broken and kicked to the side, or so I thought. Through some bad personal choices, I found myself losing just about everything. I had learned about God's Grace and I thought I knew what His grace was. Boy, was I clueless! I thought I was done in ministry and couldn't be used again. I was crushed in many ways.

One day while having breakfast with a pastor friend, he started our conversation by saying to me, "I don't know what you have gone through, that doesn't really matter to me. My job is not to judge you. We can talk about anything you want. We can talk about God, worship, music, golf, football, whatever you want to talk about. My job today is to wrap God's loving arms around you." That day, I discovered what God's Grace looked like. That breakfast changed my life in so many ways. I was accepted for who I was, and not for my short comings. I developed a level of compassion for others I had not seen before, and that compassion has served me very well, even to this day.

Sometimes the lessons we have to learn come in the form of bondage. We are all in bondage to something at some point in time. We listen to the words of others that can be detrimental to us. They can be putdowns from parents, coaches, spouses, co-workers, siblings, and many others. These words can have a lasting impact on our lives, how we think, and how we perceive ourselves.

Some of us have experienced physical or emotional abuse, and these abuses can have a lasting effect on our lives. Many times, they can stifle us to the point that we are not able to move forward with anything. They can create such fear in us that we become petrified.

What is the answer to us becoming unstuck and being able to shake off the fear?

There are many things we try to overcome such fears, some of them may work for a short period, but the effects are usually short lived. We often try journaling, counseling, exercising, meditation or substances like drugs and alcohol, but all to no avail.

The only thing I have found that works every time is to forgive the perpetrator, whether it is an individual, group, or an entity. Sometimes you even have to forgive God because you may feel as though He could have fixed the situation, or prevented it from happening at all, but He didn't. Forgiveness is not for the other person, rather, it is for **YOU**! It has been said that holding on to unforgiveness is like drinking poison and expecting the other person to die. When you forgive, it simply gives you peace of mind.

"And the peace of God, which surpasses all comprehension, will guard your hearts and your minds in Christ Jesus." Philippians 4:7

"Peace I leave with you; My peace I give to you; not as the world gives do I give to you. Do not let your heart be troubled, nor let it be fearful." John 14:27

Then there is the fact that we often don't know who we really are in God's eyes. We tend to believe the lies spoken to us by others. God sees us differently though. If you are one of His children, He sees you as sinless because of the work Jesus did on the cross. He sees us as Victors! Strong! Loving! Joyful! Content! Confident! And the list goes on.

So, the question is, *who are you*? Are you weak, or are you confident? Are you defeated, or are you a *victor*?

Are you depressed, or are you *joyful*? The choice is yours. See yourself as your Creator sees you. You are an *overcomer* because of His strength. Live in *confidence* through Christ! Tell yourself daily who you are because of what Jesus did for you on the cross. Throw away the defeatist attitude and celebrate being a new creation. *"Therefore, if anyone is in Christ, he is a new creature; the old things passed away; behold, new things have come."* 2 Corinthians 5:17

One final thought. Forgiveness and the realization of knowing who we are in God's eyes are critical for us to be able to leave our past where it belongs. Sometimes we need a booster, or a jump start though.

I remember a time when I was in a very dark place in my life. I had a cloud of depression that seemed to hover over me 24 hours a day. I simply could not shake it. One day, I was in my beautiful, spacious, one-bedroom apartment, overlooking a lush asphalt parking lot. I couldn't bear the depression any more. That was when God spoke to me. His words weren't audible, but I could sense it was Him speaking to me. He simply said, "Worship Me." My response was rather abrupt. "Not a chance, You could fix my situation." A few minutes later, again I heard, "Worship Me." Again, I said "No way!" A third time, God confronted me with, "Worship Me!!!" This time, I collapsed to my knees and started to worship Him. Instantly, the depression I had been carrying for weeks, vanished! It was gone completely, as if it was never there in the first place.

I tell you this as a sort of a silver bullet. When you are weak and weary, worship your Creator. He will sustain you and carry you. When you worship Him, you take your eyes off yourself and your problems.

Before you get to the point of debilitating depression, worship the Creator, the Giver of Life. You will be glad you did and wish you had been worshiping Him all along.

Learn to forgive early and often. Know who you are in the eyes of God, your Creator. These answers are very simple, but usually not very easy. They require action and humility on your part, but in the long run, they are worth it.

Know that you are blessed because you have been

Restored by Grace

If you have questions or want to learn more about what it means to have a personal relationship with Jesus Christ, then visit www.chataboutJesus.com

About the Author

Stephen H Reed, son, entrepreneur, worship leader, encourager, coach/counselor, and now writer and storyteller. Having grown up in a model Christian home, dad a minister, mom a school teacher, I learned a lot of life long lessons. I learned the value of work, honesty, character and integrity. I also learned that skillful communication was at the core of sharing my beliefs. As the youngest of four boys, I had to learn to make my point and make it fast or I would be left behind.

At the age of sixteen, I was confronted with the reality that my family heritage was of no value when it came to spending eternity with my Savior. It wasn't about who my parents were, it was about a personal relationship with Jesus that mattered. Coming to a saving knowledge of who Jesus is and what His grace and mercy meant to me, I started this Christian walk.

Much like James, Jesus' half-brother, my faith has grown every day as I see His hands at work. While pursuing this project and others, I have witnessed one miracle after another. I have had prayers answered before I even knew there was a prayer that needed to be raised.

As I look back on my life, I realize that I have only begun to learn who Jesus truly is and the depth of his grace and mercy.

I invite you to check out my blog and videos, order books and eBooks, or schedule me for a presentation at your church, ministry, retreat, conference, or other ministry: www.StephenReedMinistries, www.myhalfbrother.com, or www.fb.me/StephenReedMinistries. See what else is happening with the ministry.

Other work by the author

My Half Brother – A Journey of Hope and Grace

What would it be like to grow up in the household where your older brother is literally "perfect"? I'm not talking about everyone's perception, I mean "perfect", as in He never does anything wrong. So, who am I talking about? Of course, I'm talking about my big brother, Jesus. I'm James, the number two son of Joseph and Mary and this is my story of My Half Brother. Come along with me as I share stories from our childhood, teen years and then as He starts His ministry. You will see His death and resurrection like never before. Join me on this journey of hope and grace.

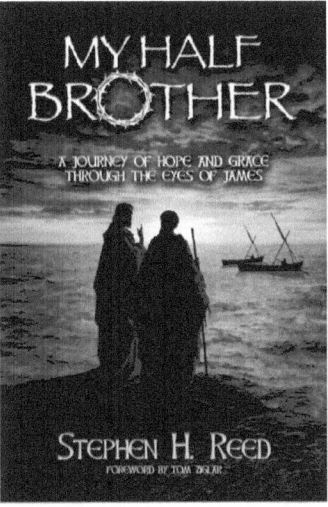

James,
a bondservant of God

"Steve has captured a truly unique view of the gospel. Can you imagine life in the shadow of the perfect big brother? This is a fresh way to renew your love for the Word of God and for Jesus Himself. You'll enjoy every page!"

Chris Machen
President, The Master's Music Company
Christian Artist & Worship Leader

Storyteller and speaker

Mr. Reed is the author of My Half Brother, A Journey of Hope and Grace, Through the Eyes of James. It is a Biblically based novel about the life of Christ from the perspective of James, Jesus' half-brother. Steve brings both a light-hearted look at Jesus' life, but also shares the amazing stories of faith and miracles from a third person's point of view. Imagine growing up in a household where your big brother is literally perfect. In fact, He is the Son of God. You would have some wild stories too if you were His Half Brother. I promise, you will enjoy this unique view of the life of Christ.

Steve's favorite thing to do these days is to dress up in his Biblical costume as James and tell the stories of his Half

Brother. He loves to share with churches, retreats, conferences and anyone else who will slow down long enough to listen.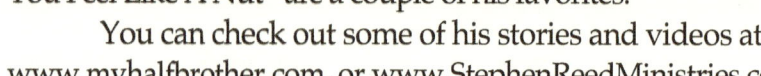

In addition to Mr. Reed's dramatic presentations, he enjoys preparing and delivering devotional messages. "Playing Hide and Seek with God" and "Sometimes You Feel Like A Nut" are a couple of his favorites.

You can check out some of his stories and videos at www.myhalfbrother.com, or www.StephenReedMinistries.com. Email me at: Info@StephenReedMinistries.com

www.ingramcontent.com/pod-product-compliance
Lightning Source LLC
Chambersburg PA
CBHW030533020726
47494CB00004B/1340